Brownlow North

The Prodigal Son

Anatiposi

Brownlow North

The Prodigal Son

Reprint of the original, first published in 1871.

1st Edition 2023 | ISBN: 978-3-38211-257-8

Anatiposi Verlag is an imprint of Outlook Verlagsgesellschaft mbH.

Verlag (Publisher): Outlook Verlag GmbH, Zeilweg 44, 60439 Frankfurt, Deutschland
Vertretungsberechtigt (Authorized to represent): E. Roepke, Zeilweg 44, 60439 Frankfurt, Deutschland
Druck (Print): Books on Demand GmbH, In de Tarpen 42, 22848 Norderstedt, Deutschland

THE PRODIGAL SON;

or,

THE WAY HOME.

BY

BROWNLOW NORTH, B.A.,

Magdalen Hall, Oxford;

Registrar of the Diocese of Winchester and Surrey.

AUTHOR OF "OURSELVES," ETC.

LONDON:

WILLIAM HUNT AND COMPANY,

Holles Street, Cavendish Square.

1871.

CONTENTS.

I.

About Prodigals.

"A certain man had two sons: and the younger of them said to his father, Father, give me the portion of goods that falleth to me. And he divided unto them his living. And not many days after the younger son gathered all together, and took his journey into a far country, and there wasted his substance with riotous living. And when he had spent all, there arose a mighty famine in that land; and he began to be in want. And he went and joined himself to a citizen of that country; and he sent him into his fields to feed swine. And he would fain have filled his belly *with the husks that the swine did eat: and no man gave unto him. And when he came to himself, he said, How many hired servants of my father's have bread enough and to spare, and I perish with hunger! I will arise and go to my father, and will say unto him, Father, I have sinned against heaven, and before thee, and am no more worthy to be called thy son: make me as one of thy hired servants. And he arose and came to his father. But when he was yet a great way off, his father saw him, and had compassion, and ran, and fell on his neck, and kissed him. And the son said unto him, Father, I have sinned against heaven, and in thy sight, and am no more worthy to be called thy son. But the father said to his servants, Bring forth the best robe, and put it on him; and put a ring on his hand, and shoes on his feet: and bring hither the fatted calf, and kill it; and let us eat, and be merry: for this my son was dead, and is alive again; he was lost, and is found. And they began to be merry.*" (Luke xv. 11—24.)

There are some passages in the Word of God, with which different men, according to their different temperaments and characteristics, think they have little to do; that however suitable they may be to others, they in no way apply to them; and that consequently they can teach them little. One such passage, I think, is the parable of the Prodigal Son.

When this parable is given out for the text of a sermon, or is the title of a book laying on the table, many think that the subject can concern them but little; that whatever else they may be, they are not Prodigal Sons; have never been guilty of his sins; of riotous living, of wasting their substance with harlots, of reducing themselves by their own misconduct to beggary, or of trying to satisfy their hunger at the swine trough. Yet have one and all of us, from the most exalted Christian to the very least, not once only, but again and again done all these things; and it is not alone for the sake of the confessed Prodigal, but for the sake of all who think they have nothing in common with him, that I have chosen the Prodigal Son for the subject of this little book.

In the fifth chapter of the Revelation it has pleased God to reveal to us the song that the redeemed sing in heaven: "Worthy is the Lamb that was slain to receive power, and riches, and wisdom, and strength, and honour, and glory, and blessing." This is the song they all sing,—all the redeemed; but every one of that great multitude—a multitude that no man can number—who now sings it before the throne of God and of the Lamb, first learned to sing it on earth. It was here on earth they not only first learned they were not their own, and had nothing they could call their own; but that even were the whole world their own, it could never make them happy. It was here on earth, taught by the Holy Ghost, they first learned that Christ, and Christ alone, was a satisfying portion; and that it was altogether worth their while to give *all that they had* for Him. The price He cost each may have differed as to earthly value; but in every case, *all that they had* was the price that each paid, and that each thought it worth his while to pay. Matthew paid it, and Peter paid it, Paul paid it, and the penitent thief paid it. In one case it may have been the rich tables of the money changer, in another the comparatively valueless nets of the poor fisherman, in the third the righteousness of a Paul, in a fourth the extenuating excuses of the sinner who had had few advantages; but the *main* fact was the same with one and all of that vast multitude,—each one had thought it worth his while to give his *all* for Christ. It was the price asked: each thought Him worth it, and so each forsook all that he had and gave it; and from that moment, but never until that moment, each begun to sing on earth what he now sings in heaven: "*Worthy is the Lamb that was slain to receive power, and riches, and wisdom, and strength, and honour, and glory, and blessing.*"

But for all this, all that multitude in heaven were Prodigal sons on earth. Again and again did they squander what they confessed was not their own, wasting their Lord's substance on lords many and gods many; again and again did they reduce themselves by their own misconduct to beggary, trying to satisfy their hungerings with the husks that the swine eat; and again and again had they to arise and go to their Father, and say, "Father, I have sinned." It is not because they were not Prodigals; but because their Father's mercies failed not, that they are now singing before the throne, "*Worthy is the Lamb that was slain to receive power, and riches, and wisdom, and strength, and honour, and glory, and blessing.*"

And are you and I better than they? No, in no wise. Do you call yourself a Christian? Then you say Christ is worthy to receive all that you have to give Him; that your power, your riches,—all and any talents that God has entrusted to you,—it is your bounden duty to employ for His honour and glory. You say so, and you believe it. But have you given to Him His due? Have you rendered unto God the things that are God's? Oh, that I could convince all who do not know it, that let their decencies, moralities, and externals of religion be what they may, if they have never felt penitence for sin as this Prodigal felt it, and arisen and gone to their Father for pardon as this Prodigal arose and went to his, their very moralities and religious observances are husks, and can never save their souls from perishing. Without one single exception, every man has done as the Prodigal did; and without one single exception, every man who has not arisen and gone to His Father is in the same position as was the Prodigal Son, when he was sitting with his back to his father's house and his face towards the swine trough.

Observe, however, that in saying these things I would on no account detract from the primary intention of the parable, which is essentially the Prodigal's parable. Our blessed Lord spoke it when all the publicans and sinners, the lowest and most degraded of the people, both men and women, drew near to hear Him; and when the Pharisees and Scribes, who trusted in themselves that they were righteous and despised others, murmured against Him, saying, "This Man receiveth sinners and eateth with them." It was to rebuke the Pharisee, and encourage sinners to come to Him, that our Lord spake the three blessed parables recorded in Luke xv.: parables so plain, and in their first and most immediate signification so easily understood, that the wayfaring man, though a fool, may read them as he runs; in height and depth, in length and breath so wide and comprehensive, that to the most lost and chief of sinners is it made plain that the door of salvation is open to them; and so marvellous in their revelations that these most lost and chief of sinners may know of a surety that if they will turn from their sins, arise and go *to their* Father, not only will that Father forgive and receive them, but that their repentance will cause joy in heaven—joy IN THE PRESENCE of the angels of God.

Oh, reader, are you unconverted? If so, you have never yet done a single action that has caused joy in heaven. Did you ever think about that? Would you not like to cause joy in heaven? I know not who you are; perhaps some great one amongst men. No matter, if you are unconverted, what I have said above is true of you: you have never done anything but grieve God's Holy Spirit, from your youth upward until now. Perhaps you are amongst the poor and needy,—almost unknown,—few, peradventure no one, caring whether you are alive or dead. No matter,—be you who or what you may amongst men, of such value are you in the sight of God, that if you will now arise and go to your Father you will cause joy in heaven. In spite of all your past, HE in whose presence the angels stand will receive you, rejoice over you, and not be ashamed to call you SON. It is meet that we should make merry and be glad, "*for this my son was dead and is alive again, he was lost and is found,*" were the words of the father on the return of the Prodigal; and while every one, not excepting the very best on earth, has occasion to arise and go to his Father, and say, "Father, I have sinned," not only the very best, but the very worst may be as sure as the Word of God can make them, that if they will arise and go, they shall receive from the Father the welcome of the Prodigal Son.

Having said thus much by way of introduction, let us go into detail; and may God, for Jesus Christ's sake, give me His Spirit to teach me what I write, and bless by the same Spirit what is written to my readers.

"*A certain man had two sons: and the younger of them said to his father, Father, give me the portion of goods that falleth to me. And he divided unto them his living. And not many days after the younger son gathered all together, and took his journey into a far country, and there wasted his substance with riotous living.*" (Luke xv. 11—13.)

I do not propose in this little book to comment on the elder of these two sons, but to endeavour to draw instruction from the history of the younger.

The younger son, we read, received his portion: the father, out of his treasures, gave him the portion of goods that fell to him.

Now as the father did to this younger son, so has God done to you and me: given us a portion,—the portion that falleth to us; God dividing to every man severally as He will. It is true we have not all received the same portion; but unless we have been born without reason, and thus not accountable beings, we have all received from God certain talents,—a certain amount of power, and riches, and wisdom, and strength, by the right employment of which we can bring honour and glory and blessing to God.

And for the right employment of these talents we are accountable to God. To give us anything with which we can serve Him is a great gift, a great condescension, a great mercy; but the gift entails a great responsibility. Many appear not to think so; many live as if there was no hereafter,—no God, no death, no account to be rendered; but unless such repent and believe the Gospel, woe to them in the day of judgment. Can any man suppose that when the father gave his portion to his younger son, he imagined that in a few days he would gather all together, leave his house, and break away from his authority? So, can any one suppose that God has endowed man with all with which He has endowed him merely to enable him to live without God in the world? The Prodigal acted as if his father had given him his portion simply to render him independent of him, and he greatly sinned against his father; and as he sinned, so sins every man, no matter how much better he may think himself than the Prodigal, who spends his portion as seems right in his own eyes, without reference to the commandments of God the Giver. I say, so sins every man; for it requires nothing more to bring us in guilty of all the charges brought against the Prodigal. He who lives for self and the things of time, rather than for God and His glory, has gathered all that he has received together, and gone as far off as he can from his Father.

In God's sight, let that man live as morally and respectably as he may, he is a squanderer and a spendthrift, wasting God's substance in riotous living.

Reader, are you such an one? Have you long been living afar from God; so long as almost to forget that HE IS? Have you got so into the habit of thinking and acting for yourself that it never enters into your head to consult the Word of Him who gave you all that you have, that you may learn how best to employ it? If so, may God forgive you, and give you wisdom, for you know not what you do. You are not only the enemy of God, man, and your own soul; but the destroyer of your present personal and immediate happiness. What was the Prodigal seeking when he left his father's house? Happiness: the same thing that you have been seeking all your life. Did he find it? No!

Have you? No! He never found it until he returned to his father; neither will you. Happiness temporal, as well as happiness eternal, *both depend on our being with our Father.* Oh, I beseech you, receive this truth. There is no true happiness away from God.

From the days of your childhood, when you sought it in sugar-plums and playthings, happiness has been your aim and object. You have done everything with reference to it. When you were a child you wanted play-things; but you gave them up, because they did not make you happy: you then sought happiness in something else; that too disappointed you, and you took to something else; and when you exchanged that for some other thing, because that too disappointed you, again you were disappointed. Some things perhaps you have desired and never got; and other things you have desired and got, only to wish you had never got them; but as you have advanced from childhood to youth, from youth to manhood, and from manhood to old age, changing with each succeeding period of life the notion of what would make you happy, have you found happiness? I know you have not. You may have felt at times the same pleasure that the Prodigal felt when he was wasting his substance in riotous living; but even you yourself will not give the name of happiness to that. Unless you have arisen and gone to your Father, I know you have not found happiness. Some one has said, one of the many proofs of our fall is, that we seek happiness in the things of earth; one of the many proofs of the original nobility of our nature is, that they never satisfy us, and "this witness is true." Never until you acknowledge you are not your own, but are bought with a price; never until you believe "Worthy is the Lamb that was slain to receive power, and riches, and wisdom, and strength;" never until you arise and go to your Father, and say, "Father, I have sinned," can you be happy: but then, from that moment, shall you not only begin to do what you have never yet done,—bring glory to God, be a blessing to man, and do good to your own soul,—but you shall be happy; you shall have in your heart the only thing worth the name, "*The peace of God which passeth all understanding.*" If you are living without Christ and without God in the world, whatever else you may have, you have not THAT PEACE; you know you have not.

"The natural man," says God, "receiveth not the things of the Spirit of God, for they are foolishness to him;" and the Prodigal, in his natural state, had no notion of the truths which I have just written. No sooner did he receive his portion than he longed to be released from control. He felt independent; the best judge of what would be for his own happiness; and his ungoverned spirit chafed under the restraints of his father's house. If he stayed there, one of the rules of that house was obedience; and obedience to his father was irksome to him; for he and his father saw things very differently, and were totally at variance as to their ideas of happiness. If he acted as his father told him he should be miserable. Why, then, now that he was rich and increased in goods, and had need of nothing,—or at all events had much goods laid up for many years—should he bear a bondage against which his heart rose in enmity? The struggle, if any, was very short: "*Not many days after, the younger son gathered all together, and took his journey into a far country.*" Poor

Prodigal: he had no eyes to see the folly of departing from his father!

And now the Prodigal is fairly off,—far, far away from the restraints of his father—no master but his own will, no counsellor but his own heart. How happy he thought himself; how independent; what a free man! How bright his prospects; how great the pleasure and enjoyment before him! He will make no tarrying; he will enter on the pleasures of his inheritance at once. The portion he has received from his father will get for him all he wants: he need deny himself nothing; there is no longer anything between him and the enjoyment of all his nature longs for. With him, who knew no will but his own, to will was to do: and from thenceforth his power, his riches, his wisdom, his strength, all that he had, and all that he was, were alike impressed into one service and employed for one object: SELF.

Reader, you most likely think the Prodigal was very foolish. His ideas of self-gratification very likely differed widely from yours. His was rioting and drunkenness, chambering and wantonness, banquettings, revellings, and such like: you, perhaps, thank God you are not like this man,—not a drunkard, or unclean, or openly profane; yet for all that your heart may be filled with pride, covetousness, love of the world, or some other of the many,—if not grosser lusts of the flesh,—yet of the lusts of the eye and the pride of life. If this be so, if your life is guided and governed by your own will, and not by the teaching of the Holy Spirit, it matters not in what road, *away from God*, your own will leads you; in God's sight you are no better than the Prodigal. You are wasting the substance that He has entrusted to you, and what happened to the Prodigal will most certainly happen to you. *You will one day not only come to want, but* FEEL IT. You have been in want all your life, but you may never have felt it yet; you were born in want; you were born as is every man, without God,—and God is the great want of man; and sooner or later, either here or hereafter, you *must* feel your want. It may never be here, but pray to God it may; for if it is here happy are you. Here there is an open door through which you may go to the Father, and like the Prodigal, get all your want supplied; but it may never be here: and if it is never here, it will be in the world to come, where you will most certainly be in want; want of a drop of water to cool your tongue. Remember when Jesus spake of wanting water, it is told us, "This spake He of the Spirit, which they that believe on Him shall receive." Then seek ye the Lord while He may be found, call ye upon Him while He is nigh. Let the wicked forsake his way, and the unrighteous man his thoughts, and let him return unto the Lord, and He will have mercy on him; and to our God, for He will abundantly pardon. You must forsake your own *thoughts*, as well as your own ways.

We will speak of the Prodigal's want in the next chapter.

II.

About Idolaters.

"*And when he had spent all, there arose a mighty famine in that land; and he began to be in want.*" (Luke xv. 14.)

"Amongst the gods there is none like unto Thee, O God," saith David. And he gives us this reason, amongst many: that whilst "their sorrows shall be multiplied that hasten after another god" (Ps. xvi. 4), "they that seek the LORD shall not want any good thing." (Psalm xxxiv. 10.) Thus there is this difference between the LORD God and other gods: that while His worshippers, no matter what they may think, are always in the very best position in which He can place them, lacking nothing that is really good; all other gods, though they may give at the moment the thing their worshippers desire, invariably in the long run, bring them to want. Some sooner, some later; but there never was a worshipper of any but the God and Father of our Lord and Saviour Jesus Christ, who did not, at some time or other, like the Prodigal, *come to want.* "He that hath ears to hear let him hear."

There are lords many and gods many, and every man is a worshipper of some God. It is true that all gods except the LORD are the work of men's hands,—man-made gods; but for that very reason, because men have made them so, they are gods,—gods of this world: and the man who has not the LORD for his God, has no other. Some have a notion that because now we do not make an image of wood or stone, bow down to it and worship it, that idolatry at least has ceased out of the land; but I believe firmly that no heathen nation in the darkest ages of superstition, ever made, bowed down to, or worshipped more false gods than are made, bowed down to, and worshipped by professing Christians in this nineteenth century. I know of no lust of the flesh, no lust of the eye, no pride of life, which has not been made an idol of by man, bowed down to, and worshipped.

In proof of what I havé written let us compare God's account of the idolater, as given in Isaiah, with the conduct of multitudes in our own day. "He heweth him down cedars, and taketh the cypress and the oak, which he strengtheneth for himself among the trees of the forest: he planteth an ash, and the rain doth nourish it. Then shall it be for a man to burn: for he will take thereof, and warm himself; yea, he kindleth it and baketh bread;

yea, he maketh a god, and worshippeth it; he maketh it a graven image, and falleth down thereto. He burneth part thereof in the fire; with part thereof he eateth flesh; he roasteth roast, and is satisfied: yea, he warmeth himself, and saith, Aha, I am warm, I have seen the fire: and the residue thereof he maketh a god, even his graven image: he falleth down unto it, and worshippeth it, and prayeth unto it, and saith, Deliver me; for thou art my god." (Isa. xliv. 14—17.)

Now if we substitute for this god of wood an image of gold, where is the difference between this idolater and hosts of so called Christians in the present day. He sought the cedar tree, the cypress, and the oak, as multitudes seek wealth, and for the same object. He sought, that with part he might attend to the immediate comforts of the body,—roast flesh, say, "Aha, I am warm, I have seen the fire;" and with the residue make a god. They seek that with part they may attend to the immediate comforts of the body,—roast flesh, say, "Aha, I am warm, I have seen the fire;" and with the residue make a god. Where is the difference? and yet how many, having made a fortune, bought an estate, built a house, and filled it with what their souls lusted after, are now saying to their thousands, or tens of thousands, or hundreds of thousands, what this man said to his idol of wood: "Thou art my God; in the day of my trouble thou shalt deliver me!" Do not the words of the Lord, addressed by Isaiah to the worshipper of the idol of wood, apply to this worshipper of the idol of gold: "*He feedeth on ashes: a deceived heart hath turned him aside, that he cannot deliver his soul, or say, Is there not a lie in my right hand?*" (Isa. xliv. 20.) Thus saith the Lord, "He that trusteth in his riches shall fall." Sooner or later his god *must* and *will* fail him; like the Prodigal, he shall surely come to want. (Prov. xi. 28.)

Or let us take the case of two other worshippers of the gods of this world: the highest and the lowest perhaps of all the earthly gods,—the worshippers of the gods of pleasure and of high moral and social position. By the worshipper of the god of pleasure,—too many, alas, of which there are,—I mean the sensualist: he who has no higher idea of happiness than the beasts that perish; and by the worshipper of the god of position, he whose ambition is a good name and fame, and to be highly esteemed and looked up to among the sons of men. Both these gods demand sacrifice; indeed there is no god, whether the God of heaven or among the gods of earth, who does not demand sacrifice from his worshippers. His you are to whom *you* yield yourself servant to obey.

(Rom. vi. 16.) And the proof of who is our God, is to whom do we do sacrifice?

Look at that youth, the worshipper of the god of pleasure: how he sacrifices to his god, and his god is doing all he can for him! What a gay, merry fellow he appears: full of life and high spirits, without a sorrow or a care. How many of his young acquaintances envy his enjoyments; his emancipation from the drudgery of self-control and discipline; although (and well is it for them that it is so) they dare not make the sacrifices his god requires. He works very hard for his god; especially does he try to bring him other worshippers. See him when he meets his acquaintance, the man who is worshipping position: how he urges him to make some sacrifice to the god of pleasure. "Brother," says he, "you must be very dull: come with me, if it is only for this evening; and let us eat, and drink, and be merry. The theatre and the dancing-saloon are the places for happiness; the race-course, the card-table, and the billiard-room, the places to make a rapid fortune. Come and smoke, come and drink, come and do anything you like: only come with me, and we will have a merry time together." But the worshipper of position knows better. It might be all pleasant enough while it lasted, but he has something besides pleasure to attend to: he has his character to think of; those under whose orders he is, to please; his way to make in the world; and for the sake of a momentary gratification he will not do what might injure—perhaps blight—his future prospects for life. He says, "I will not go;" and they part: one to his pleasure, and the other to his business. It was impossible they could walk together, for their gods were not the same.

A few months, or at the most a very few years after this,—for no one can stand long the sacrifice of constitution required by this most cruel of all gods, the god of pleasure; see his worshipper laid low upon the bed of sickness and of death. As he looks back upon the past, and forward to the future, what can the god of pleasure do for him? *Has he not brought him to want?* Where is the good name with which he started in life? where the means, by the right use of which he might have got on in the world? where the once healthy and vigorous constitution? where the prospects of an independent and happy old age? where his friends, where his parents? His god would still do anything for him he could, but what can he do? Unless, through grace and mercy, he yet changes his god and flies for refuge to the Lord Jesus Christ, cut down in the *midst of his days* there is no more pleasure for him either in time or in eternity. He is dying: his days of pleasure have come to an end on earth, and there is no pleasure in hell.

Let us now look at the worshipper of position. How different his career! From its beginning he is a man who makes high principle and rectitude his guide. Never was he known to tell a falsehood, or deceive, or do aught that would not bear strict scrutiny. His word has become as good as his bond; he is respected by all who know him; whether those over him or under him, one and all look up to him and trust him. He commenced life perhaps with small beginnings, but by industry and strict attention to his calling he has become rich: rich beyond his expectation. But riches do not satisfy him now: he wants something still. He has worshipped his god faithfully, and his god has done great things for him; but he might do something more, and he will aim at getting something more. Let us assume that he succeeds. The wealth that he has amassed by honest industry is great, so also is the respect in which he is held by all. The membership for the county is vacant: he stands for it, and is returned. The daughter of a neighbouring nobleman accepts him, and he is married. Nobility is offered him, and, according to his fancy, he accepts or rejects it. Royalty comes and visits him.

Is there anything left for his god to do for him? He hardly knows! He has had uninterrupted health through life, but he is getting old: he is past seventy, and the thought begins to intrude itself, that he has little time left to enjoy what he has got. He has been wanting and getting all his life, and he has little more to want or get from this world; but he has A WANT still: he wants to keep what he has got. He has laid up treasure for himself on earth, and his heart is with his treasure: he does not like to think of leaving it; he wants to stay where his heart is. The god he has worshipped has done a great deal for him, but he cannot help him here: his power was only for the earth, and no earthly power can supply what he now needs. The god that this man worshipped, as did the god of pleasure, has brought his worshipper to WANT!

Ah, reader, glance at this man on his death-bed! Is he not as poor, wretched, naked, and needy, as was the dying worshipper of the god of pleasure? By uprightness and moral rectitude, by the sacrifice of pleasure to principle, by self-denial through life, he has attained, and justly, to a high position amongst men; his god to whom he sacrificed has done for him what he could. As the worshipper of pleasure got his pleasure, so this worshipper of position has got his position; and great, very great, is the difference between what the one got and the other. The one got so little, and the other so much of what the world can give, that it is scarcely speaking too strongly to say, that one lost and the other gained the whole world! But what shall it profit a man if he gains the whole world, and loses his own soul? Far, far be it from me to say that there is no difference between the worshipper of pleasure and the worshipper of position; so far as this world is concerned there is all the difference: all the difference between happiness and misery; self-respect and self-loathing; every evil and every good. Yet when these two worshippers come to their last sickness; when the doctor puts his hand upon their pulse, and tells them they must die; are you infidel enough to say they are not both equally in want? If a man can be saved by moral and upright conduct, then they are not; but if his own probity and uprightness—if his doing his duty to himself and his neighbour, cannot atone for forgetfulness and neglect of God—if, in short, what Paul says is true, that by the deeds of the law no flesh shall be justified,—then, however great was the difference between them here—however reprobate the one and however much all that man could love or desire the other,—when they approach the same end—DEATH—they both are in want, and they both have the same want. They both of them are in need of what neither of them ever sought, or thought worth seeking,—God—Christ—the Holy Spirit—the Blood that cleanseth from all sin—and the Obedience in which a man can stand before God and be made righteous.

I have said that the worship of high, moral, and social position is the highest form of creature worship, but perhaps I am wrong;

for after all it is but the highest and most worldly-wise form of unmixed self-worship. The heart of man, and more especially I think the heart of woman, is capable of rising out of self-worship altogether, and of living as wholly and totally for another, as any man ever lived for himself. This worship, however, because it worships and serves the creature more than the Creator, must, like all other creature worships, end in misery and want. It is always idolatry—sometimes perhaps very beautiful idolatry—as the adoration of a wife, a husband, a parent, a child; or I will add—because I think I may warn and do good—the adoration of a maiden for her betrothed, or some other object lawful to be loved: but when once love passes the bounds prescribed by God, it is a breach of the first commandment—becomes idolatry—and is called in Scripture "*Inordinate affection.*" I know I have ventured above to say that this affection is sometimes very beautiful; but harsh as I may appear for saying it, it is only so to the natural eye of man: it is classed by God amongst *the most abominable sins*—as one of those things for which "*the wrath of God cometh on the children of disobedience.*" (Coloss. iii. 5, 6.) God is a jealous God, and will not give His glory to another: He seeth not as man seeth, and what is highly esteemed amongst men is abomination in His sight. Heaven and earth shall pass away, but Christ's word shall not pass away; and that declares—as every child in the country knows—He that loveth father or mother more than Me, is not worthy of Me. He that loveth wife or children, brethren or sisters, yea, or his own life more than Me, cannot be my disciple.

Not only under the New Testament, but under the Old; not only under the Christian dispensation, but since the world began, has THIS been the truth of God: *that the creature worshipper, let his worship take what form it may, has the curse of God resting on him.* What I say may sound strange and strong language, to many but it is true; for, "*Thus saith the Lord, Cursed be the man that trusteth in man, and maketh flesh his arm, and whose heart departeth from the Lord. For he shall be like the heath in the desert and shall not see when good cometh; but shall inherit the parched places in the wilderness, in a salt land, and not inhabited.*" (Jerem. xvii. 5.) Not only in our day, but since the world began, how many broken hearts, deceived, desolated, disappointed in, or deserted by their idol, *have felt the power of this curse.* It is on them—it is in them—and fly from it as they may, it follows them. In the crowded assembly or the solitary chamber it is the same; as is the heath in the desert, so is everything around and about them—desert; the world is to them a wilderness, and they themselves are as a parched place. They have a heart that can love and worship, but they have no object to love and worship: they have lost their idol, and they have no God. Their inner man is as a land sown with salt: their soul is blank, empty, not inhabited.

Reader, does your heart tell you you have been an idol worshipper? The curse saith that "such shall not see when good cometh;" and what is to become of you if that curse remaineth on you. Your eyes will remain blinded, and you will never see good,—will never see God. Good has come to you at this moment; yea, God Himself has come; for God and good are One, and there is none good but One, and that is God. He has come to *you to put* you in mind, by the instrumentality of this little book, of the curse that is on the idolater, and to urge you by the warnings of that curse to give up your idol. If you will give up your idol, and turn to Him, He will repent Him of the evil pronounced against you. His Word is pledged to do so, for thus saith the Lord: "At what instant I shall speak concerning a nation, and concerning a kingdom to pluck up, and to pull down and to destroy it, if that nation against whom I have pronounced turn from their evil, I will repent of the evil that I thought to do unto them." (Jer. xviii. 7, 8.) Now if against a nation, then against an individual; and if your heart accuses you of the idolatry, and you feel that you are under its curse, open it at once to Him who now offers Himself to you, and He will come in and dwell with you, and supply all your need.

Continue to cling to your idol, or the remembrance of your idol, and you must want for ever; want in "the pit wherein is no water;" but accept Christ and turn to God, and instead of emptiness there shall be fulness; instead of curse, there shall be blessing; the parched ground shall become a pool, and the thirsty land springs of water. Instead of the thorn shall come up the fir tree, and instead of the briar shall come up the myrtle tree; the wilderness and the solitary place shall be glad, and the desert shall rejoice and blossom as the rose. (Zech. ix. 11; Isai. xxxv. 1; xxxv. 7; and lv. 13.)

In conclusion, I repeat—no matter what the form of the idolatry—that he who spends his power, his riches, his wisdom, his strength on any earthly thing, squanders God's substance, and like the Prodigal, will some day find that he has spent all—that there is a mighty famine—and that he is IN WANT.

III.

About the Sheep and the Swine.

"*And he went and joined himself to a citizen of that country; and he sent him into his fields to feed swine. And he would fain have filled his belly with the husks that the swine did eat; and no man gave unto him.*" (Luke xv. 15, 16.)

The Prodigal was in want! He had always been in want, but this was want that made itself felt. Before this he had been able in a sense to supply his need; but he could do nothing to supply it now, and he felt it. He was in want when he left his father—but he relieved it by gathering all together and going away into a far country: he was in want again in the far country,—the mere fact of being his own master soon lost its novelty; he required something more to satisfy him, and was again in want. Pleasures and amusements supplied this, and he wasted his substance: still he was unsatisfied; and pleasure quickly grew into dissipation, and dissipation into riotous living. It was not until he had spent all,—until he had tried and exhausted all that he could conceive of earthly gratification, and found it unsatisfying,—that there arose a dearth in his heart, and *he felt* that he was in want.

It is a solemn time for poor needy man when first he feels himself in want; first feels that the world and the things of the world can never satisfy him. I believe that this happens to many before they are very old: and happy is he who, the first time he feels it, arises and goes to his Father. He who waits for a second or a third warning will certainly entail upon himself much misery,—very likely *everlasting destruction.*

When a man is brought to believe that the things of this world can never satisfy him, he is in a sense under the teaching of the Spirit of God. When such a thought comes to a man, it is wisdom, it is truth, it is that knowledge which is the gift of God; and woe to him who, in spite of God's teaching, continues to seek in any other thing a satisfying portion. One of two things will certainly happen to him: *God will either smite him, or let him alone;* either strike him with some heavy blow, and bring him, as He did the Prodigal, into deep affliction; or, swearing in His wrath that he shall never enter into His rest, cease to strive with him by His Holy Spirit. In that case, like the workers of iniquity, he may prosper in the world, but it will be the prosperity of fools, which destroys them. (Prov. i. 32.)

"A brutish man," that is, man in his natural state, says David, "knoweth not, neither doth a fool understand this.—When the wicked do spring as the grass, and all the workers of iniquity do flourish, it is that they shall be destroyed for ever" (Ps. xcii. 6, 7): and there can be no doubt that there are many people now on earth who once felt a desire for something better than anything the world can give, who have not only long since lost the desire, but *will never feel it again.* The cares of this world, and the deceitfulness of riches, and the lusts of other things have entered in and choked the desire; and in their anxiety for the body, they have ceased to remember, or perhaps believe, they have a soul. They have been *let alone of God.* If so, they may never again know much of earthly care or trouble; they may live in peace and comfort till they are old and grey-headed: but *their end* will be everlasting destruction. They will never again feel spiritual want, never again be troubled about God and their souls, until they stand before God in judgment. THEN THEY WILL. Oh, brother, be wise in time.

If, however, as was the case with the Prodigal, a man is one who God is determined not to lose, if that man does not give himself to Him without a blow, the blow will surely come. He will not allow him to prosper afar off from Himself: He loves him too well, and is stronger than he. All he has got he has received from Him, and He has given him *nothing*, employ it as he may, that can satisfy him apart from Himself. If he tries to make his portion his god, he soon exhausts all that it can do for him, and comes to felt want; and when that moment of felt want arrives on earth, it is a moment of moments for the poor Prodigal: let him arise and go at once to his Father.

Oh, who can tell the importance of that moment to a man when for the first time in his life he feels he should like to be a Christian! What misery would he have saved himself, and what grief to the Spirit of his Father, if, when first he felt in want, the Prodigal had arisen and gone back. He had to do it in the end, and so has every child of Adam, or perish; but what sin, and shame, and sorrow it would have saved him, if he had done it at the first! But no: the heart of man is desperately wicked and deceitful above all things; and the desperately wicked heart rebelled against going back; and the deceitful heart taught, that even bond-service with a citizen of the far off country, would be more tolerable than the duties of a son in the house of his father.

I believe there is nothing the natural heart of man hates so much as the idea of returning to God. The Prodigal was in want: he must do *something* to supply it, and all his own means were gone. Should he go back to his father, or toil out a miserable existence without hope or aim, in bond-service in the far country? The history tells us how he decided: "*he went and joined himself to a citizen of that country.*"

If you who are reading this book have ever felt your need of Christ, and yet are still trying to supply your need with the things of this world, arise and go to God at once. If you do not, either the blow will come, or He will *let you alone.*

From the moment the Prodigal decided to remain in the far country, it was line upon line, precept upon precept. The hand of his father was against him—in love it is true—but still against him—and his position became worse and worse. "*Behold I am against thee*" is an awful scripture, yet it occurs very often in the Bible; and not only is the hand of God against the reprobate—against those who are given up and let alone—but against every man who, feeling himself to be a wanting, needy creature, endeavours to supply his wants with anything that is not God. If God be for us, who can be against us? but if God be against us, who can be for us? Vain, then, is all human aid; vain the help of any citizen of this country. If God be against us, utterly vain and worse than useless is every device and plan of man to do good to himself.

By joining himself to a citizen of this country the Prodigal made his position worse than ever: *he sent him into his fields to feed swine!*

No son of the Father ever yet joined himself to a citizen of this country who did not send him into his fields to feed swine.

Let me try and explain what I mean.

The world is divided into two classes, and only two: the children of God and the children of the wicked one—the clean and the unclean,—the sheep and the swine. Those who are washed in the Blood of the Lord Jesus Christ are the sheep—the clean,—the children of God; those who are not washed in the blood of the Lord Jesus Christ are the swine—the unclean,—the children of the wicked one. There is no middle or third class: the devil teaches many that there is; but that is the devil's teaching: the Bible says there is not. And not only does every body belong to one or other of the two classes mentioned, but from every one of us there is an influence constantly going forth, which is *feeding* sheep or feeding swine,—an *influence* which has a power for good or evil over those with whom we associate, and which is helping forward the cause, either of God or the devil in the world. "He who is not with Me is against Me," says the Lord Jesus; and he whose religion is a merely negative religion—a religion hid under a bushel,—a religion from which nothing springs calculated to do positive good—is starving the cause of God in the world, and feeding swine.

Now whenever a citizen of the far off country gets hold of a child that has wandered away from his Father, he invariably, as I have said before, sends him into his fields to feed swine; sends him to associate with, at the best a mixed multitude, amongst whom he will allow him to scatter nothing but husks. No matter in what station of life it may be—in the palace or public house, it is one and the same thing; if he who has joined himself to a citizen of this country habitually endeavours to scatter that which can nourish and feed sheep, it will soon be settled for him whether or not he shall continue in the service of the citizen. So long as he scatters nothing but what the swine feed on, the citizen delights in him: he is amongst his most valued servants; for well he knows there is no one who does better service to the cause of the swine master than a son of the Father scattering husks. But the son of the Father cannot feed sheep while in the service of the citizen of this country; for the citizen will not keep such a servant in his house.

The man who mixes with the world may say what he will, but he *must* put forth the things of the world: let him mix with the world, and attempt to put forth the things of God, and the world will separate *from him.* And I believe this should be the true cause of a Christian's separation: not that he has refused to associate with the world; but that having been in it—as not of it, but as trying to do good to it,—*the world has refused to associate with him.* I have seen a man refuse to get into a railway carriage with another who he thought would be likely to speak to him about his soul.

Yet how many are there who—because charity hopeth all things—we would hope are sons of the Father, who never seem to serve God in the world, and are thus certainly serving the swine master. Many perhaps do it without thinking about it, though that is no excuse; and whether they think about it or not, it is a fact, that every Christian who mixes with the people of this world, without making his Christianity *known and felt*, feeds swine. The people with whom he mixes, no matter whether for business or pleasure, are perishing: they are in spiritual destitution—

in want, which the husks on which they feed (the things of this world) can never supply nor satisfy; and he professes to have the true bread, of which if a man eat he shall never hunger; yet not only does he never offer them this bread, but in their presence at least, never seems to feed on it himself. The only things on which they ever see him feed are the husks on which they themselves feed; the only things they ever see him scatter are the husks that they themselves scatter. Verily is not such a man feeding swine? verily does he not look very like one of the herd? Who could have recognised a son of the Father in the poor Prodigal when he was trying to satisfy his hunger with the husks the swine eat?

How many try to relieve the wants of the soul, by feeding on husks! "I cannot be always thinking of religion," said a young man to himself, who about twelve months before had professed to believe in the Lord Jesus Christ, and come out from the world. "For more than a year now I have been trying to be a Christian, and I find myself no better. I begin to think I have been wrong in separating myself so entirely from my old friends and their amusements. I am getting quite dull and melancholy, and that cannot be true religion. I wonder whether a game of billiards would do me good? There is no harm in a game of billiards. I know there is to be a great match to-night, and I am half inclined to go and see it. I am sure to meet A. and B. and C. there, and a good laugh with A. would be just the thing to cheer me up. I really think I have been going further than God requires me to go, and as I said at first, one cannot be always thinking about religion."

The thoughts passing in the mind of this

young man, will explain what I mean by trying to relieve the wants of the soul by feeding on husks. He had taken up a profession of religion, but religion had not satisfied him. After a year of trial, there was still a vacuum in his heart, and he was in want. He had no idea in his own mind at the time, however, of giving up religion, only he thought that he had been religious over much, and that to go back a little into the same sort of society, and enjoy the same amusements in moderation that he used to mix in and enjoy before he began to think about it, would be a help to him rather than a hindrance. The real thought in his heart was—though I doubt whether he even knew it himself—*if I could only get a little society in which God, and the things of God, are neither talked about nor thought of, it would make religion much pleasanter.* To such a thought there is but one answer: "Get thee behind me Satan, for thou savourest not the things that be of God." That which this young man proposed to himself was poison, not medicine; and he who in search of food for an unsatisfied soul, goes to seek it—however innocent they may be in themselves—in scenes of earthly pleasure and amusement, is an exact picture of the prodigal son trying to satisfy his hunger with the husks the swine were eating.

"*One cannot be always thinking about religion.*" Let the man or woman be sure, in whose heart is such a sentiment as this, that it is not because he has *too much*, but because he has *too little religion*, that he is dissatisfied. Only reflect for a moment. In the grace of our Lord Jesus Christ, the love of God, and the fellowship and communion of the Holy Ghost is there not enough to satisfy? Dare any man say or think that to this must be added a little of the pleasures of the world? "Love not the world," says God, "neither the things of the world. If any man love the world, the love of the Father is not in him." And again: "How long halt ye between two opinions? If the Lord be God, follow Him; but if Baal, then follow him." And again: "No man *can* serve two masters." Dear reader, if you are one of those whom religion does not satisfy, is it not clear to you that it must be more of God, more of Christ,. more of the Holy Spirit, more, in short, of true vital religion that you require, not less? There *is* enough in Christ to satisfy not only angels, and the innumerable company of the spirits of just men made perfect, but GOD HIMSELF; and that not for time only, but for eternity: and will you believe the devil's lie, that there is not enough in Him to satisfy *you?* Will you try and make perfect *His* finished work by adding to it the things of this world? Mind that I am now expressing no opinion as to whether it is right or wrong for a Christian to mix in what are called the innocent pleasures and amusements of the citizens of this world. If he is a happy Christian, strong in his Lord, and the power of His might, and will take the opportunity to be about his Master's business, let him go if he has a mind—and let him go again if he is asked; but what I DO say is, that for a person who has sought Christ *and has not as yet found in Him a satisfying portion*, to seek to make Him more satisfying by adding in the smallest degree any *earthly thing* to Christ, is to do what the Prodigal did when he left his Father's house in search of happiness; and will probably entail on him, if not a worse, at least a like experience.

You say then what am I to do? I have

sought Christ for a month, or a year, or I know not how long, and yet I have not found in Him a satisfying portion. I ask you, in return, Have you laid hold of Him *by faith?* You say you have sought Him, but have you *believed on Him?* You have gone to Him with prayers and supplications; but from whence have you taken *the answers to your prayers?* HE has said, and you know it, "Him that cometh to Me, I will in no wise cast out." Then have you, regardless of the teaching of your own natural heart, which invariably disbelieves and contradicts Christ, believed, on the faith of His Word, that He has received and accepted YOU, *because He said He would?* Christ is the great ALPHA, the BEGINNING of all religion; and if you have only sought Him, but not found Him,—have only *asked Him* to forgive and save you, but have not *believed* His written and recorded answer to that prayer,—you have not *begun* true religion yet—and no wonder you are still in want, and crying out, "What am I to do?" There is but one thing for you to do, and until you do it, you not only never can be satisfied, but never can be saved; you must BELIEVE IN THE LORD JESUS CHRIST. God shuts you up to it with the awful words, "HE THAT BELIEVETH NOT SHALL BE DAMNED;" and no matter who or what you contradict,—your reason, your senses, your wisdom, your feelings—the hearing of your ears, or the seeing of your eyes,—you *must* believe in Him, or perish. But *believe in Him;* believe neither spirit, soul, nor body,—nothing external or internal that contradicts Him; but believe in Him ONLY, and you shall find in Him a satisfying portion. "My God shall supply all your need, according to His riches in glory by Christ Jesus." (Philip iv. 19.)

But remember that Christ Jesus is the Teacher as well as the Saviour of His people; and that believing in Him, or laying hold of Him by faith, includes belief in what *He teaches*, as well as in what *He promises*. The distinguishing mark of the true Christian is not merely that he professes to believe in Jesus, but that he evidences his faith by his conduct; Christ has become his Teacher; and he no longer walks in the imaginations of his own heart, but *he walks by faith*. "Not every-one who saith unto Me, Lord, Lord, shall enter into the kingdom of heaven, but he that doeth the will of my Father which is in heaven." "He that cometh to Me, and heareth my sayings and doeth them, is like a man that built his house upon a Rock; but he that heareth my sayings and doeth them not, is like a man that built his house upon the sands." "Come unto Me all ye that labour and are heavy laden, and I will give you rest." "Take my yoke upon you, and learn of Me, and ye shall find rest unto your souls." These are all the words of Jesus, and the promise in this last quotation is positive. Christ says "*ye shall;*" but the command explains the promise: it is made to those *who take His yoke, and learn of Him.* Do you think that a soul disquieted and in search of rest can be said to be bearing Christ's yoke, or learning of Him, who seeks relief and peace in the things of this world, or in the society of its God-forgetting citizens?

If religion does not make you happy without the things of the world, I say again it is not because there is not enough in religion to satisfy you, but because YOU have not got *enough of religion.* "Acquaint thyself now with God, and be at peace," is the prescription given by God Himself, the Good Physician, to those who are in search of happiness; and the happiest man at this moment on earth, is the man who knows most of God. We become acquainted with God *by faith;* by faith in His written Word—and all men, says the Apostle, *have not faith.* Now when a man is without faith he knows nothing of God, he does not even really believe that "HE IS;" he says in his heart, "*there is no God;*" and in this state of course he can neither know nor please God. "Without faith it is impossible to please Him; for he that cometh to God must believe that He is." (Heb. xi. 6.) This is the lowest grain of faith,—have you got it? A man without faith is spiritually dead; but when faith comes, life comes: and where there is real faith and real life, there follows of necessity *the life of faith.* Faith first, and then the life of faith,—after that,—but never till that—happiness.

Now to seek relief in the things of the world

for the wants of the soul, though pleasanter at the moment to the natural man, so far from leading to acquaintance with God, which is happiness,—leads away from Him, which is misery,—and is not *the life of faith;* on the contrary, it is the certain death of anything that looks like faith. The life of faith is an up-hill, self-denying, flesh-crucifying life, with steps and stages clearly marked out by God. He who lives this life, sustains it not with the husks of this world, but with "the BREAD which came down from heaven," and with "every word that proceedeth out of the mouth of God." It leads to much from which the natural man shrinks; but never to a cross, or a bitter cup which a loving Father does not know all about. He who took up His Cross, and drank the cup His Father put into His hand, is ever beside those who live the life of faith. And this life, and this life only, as I have said before, leads *to happiness.* It leads to the cross and the bitter cup, but it leads past these, to life and peace: it leads out of what we are, into what we ought to be—it leads to the knowledge of God and His Son Jesus Christ, which is "joy unspeakable and full of glory."

Listen to the Apostle Peter addressing those who had obtained *faith*, and were now about to begin *the life of faith.*

"*Grace and peace be multiplied unto you,*" he says, "*through the knowledge of God and of Jesus our Lord.*" (2 Peter i. 1, 2.) This is my prayer for you, that grace and peace may be multiplied unto you; but this can only be "*through the knowledge of God, and of Jesus our Lord.*" Now strive together with me in my prayers to God for you. Strive not by word only, but by deed and in truth. This do: "*Giving all diligence, add to your faith virtue;*" or, as the word more correctly signifies, courage or martial valour: and to courage, "*knowledge; and to knowledge, temperance; and to temperance, patience; and to patience, godliness; and to godliness, brotherly-kindness; and to brotherly-kindness, charity. For if these things be in you, and abound, they make you that ye shall be neither barren nor unfruitful in the knowledge of our Lord Jesus Christ.*"

Let he who professeth faith evidence it by giving all diligence to *add to his faith* these things; it will be flesh crucifying, and the blessing may seem to tarry—but though the blessing may seem to tarry, the promise is sure, "*for the mouth of the Lord hath spoken it.*" These things shall make him who adds them to his faith, that he shall be neither barren nor unfruitful in the only knowledge that maketh happy,—the knowledge of our Lord Jesus Christ.

IV.

About Demoniacs.

"WHEN HE CAME TO HIMSELF." Oh, the mercy and goodness of God! The poor Prodigal came at last to himself. How much more likely it seemed when we saw him deliberately choose the service of the swine-master, that he would live and die in his madness, trying to satisfy his hunger with the husks the swine eat. "*The heart of the sons of men is full of evil,*" says Solomon, "*and madness is in their heart while they live, and after that they go to the dead.*" An awful yet an exact picture given us by God Himself, both of *the here and the hereafter* of every child of Adam who lives and dies without having *come to himself*.

But the Prodigal *did* come to himself; and though it is true that multitudes who have chosen the swine-trough perish at the swine-trough, yet nothing is too hard for God; and a man may have done what the Prodigal did—or in his own mind what he believes to be a great deal worse,—and yet come to himself. The Prodigal "CAME TO HIMSELF," and it is recorded for our learning,—recorded that NO SINNER should despair.

"WHEN HE CAME TO HIMSELF." What a volume of teaching is there in these few words! Until that moment the acts of the Prodigal had been the acts of a demoniac: he had been beside himself—out of his right mind—devil-possessed—mad.

Every man who tries to satisfy himself with anything that is not God, is mad. He is worse than mad: he is, as I have said of the Prodigal, not merely a maniac, but a demoniac.

But of that hereafter. At present I will content myself with saying he is mad. He does not think so: no madman ever does. On the contrary, he thinks those mad that think him mad. Nevertheless, no poor lunatic in his asylum, indulging in all the false fancies of his reason-bereft brain, was ever more mad, or more worthy of the pity of those who are in their right minds,—than is the man who seeks his happiness in the things of this world, and tries to satisfy himself with anything that is not God.

It has always been a disputed point between the children of God and the children of this world, which of them were in their right minds: each have always called the other mad. The Bible, both old and New Testament, is full of this. When "the young man, even the young man the prophet," anointed Jehu king over Israel, and spake to him the word of the Lord, he was called a "mad fellow." (2 Kings ix. 4.) When Isaiah wrote of his times, he said, "Truth faileth, and he that departeth from evil is accounted mad." (Isa. lix. 15, marg. reading.) When Shemaiah was in captivity in Babylon, he sent letters to all the people that were at Jerusalem, and to Zephaniah the priest, and to all the priests, to say that the Lord had made him priest, and that Jeremiah was mad, and should be put in prison and in the stocks, for which lie God punished him. (Jer. xxix. 25—32.) In the days of Hosea, the prophet was looked upon as a fool, and the spiritual man, or, as it is in the Hebrew, the man of the Spirit, as mad. (Hos. ix. 7.) In the New Testament times the conclusions of the world, not only as regarded the Lord's people, but as regarded the Lord Himself, were the same. Festus told Paul he was mad; John the Baptist they said had a devil; and while His very friends and relations could believe nothing better of the Lord Jesus than that He was "beside Himself," the Jews said, and in so saying boasted that they well said, "Thou art a Samaritan, and hast a devil, and art mad."

Now what the people thought and said in that day of Christ and His disciples, they in the spirit if not in the very letter, think and say of them still; for the opinions of the world and the maxims of the world are the same in all ages. Men and women as a body, no more believe in the Lord Jesus Christ now, than they did when He was on the earth. If He was here, they would say of Him what they did say of Him when He was here; and they do say it of His people, and our Lord warned them that they would. "The disciple is not above his Master," said Jesus. "If they *have called* the Master of the house Beelzebub, how much more shall they call them of His household?" The more a man reflects the image of Christ in this world, the more is he considered by its people a visionary—an enthusiast—mad.

But what the people of this world say and think of Christians, Christians think and know to be true of the people of the world: that *they are mad.* And not only so, but as the Jews clearly defined the particular sort of madness which they believed possessed our Lord, John the Baptist, and others of His disciples, so has God clearly defined the madness which possesses all who are not Christ's people. It is not merely the madness that is maniacal—the madness that can only destroy natural reason, and after has no further power; but it is the madness that is demoniacal,—the madness that deprives of spiritual wisdom and spiritual understanding,—the madness that brings under strong delusion to believe a lie,—the madness that destroys the soul. It is the madness wrought in "*those that are lost*," *by the god of this world*—who God tells us "*hath blinded the minds of them that believe not, lest the light of the glorious Gospel of Christ, who is the Image of God, should shine unto them.*" (2 Cor. iv. 4.)

Thus saith the Lord, and therefore, thus it is true. Can there then be a more awful delusion—a more terrible madness than that under which they labour whose minds are blinded by the god of this world? Can anything be more true of THEM than what the Jews said of our Lord: "*Thou art mad, and hast a devil*"?

I believe there is nothing more offensive to those who are not Christ's people, than to profess to believe there is a devil at all; unless, indeed, it is to add to it that they are all possessed by him. Yet it is as sure as that there is a God, and that His Word is truth, that there is a devil—that he is the prince of this world—and that he rules and reigns in the hearts of his people. "*The whole world lieth in the wicked one*," says St. John: a truth more terrible than our minds can comprehend. Yet as it is TRUTH it is best to believe it, and face it, and seek a way of deliverance; for it is not more true that as Christ could say of His people, who are not of the world, "*Ye in Me and I in you*," so Satan can say of his people, who are those that are of the world, "*Ye in me and I in you.*" Paul says, "Jesus Christ is in you, except ye be reprobates" (2 Cor. xv. 5); and let it stir up the enmity of man's heart as it may, he may be as sure as he is of the truth of God, that the man who is not "*the habitation of God through the Spirit*," is the habitation of "*the prince of the power of the air*, *the spirit that now worketh in the children of disobedience.*" (Eph. ii. 2.)

Men for the most part seem to forget that Satan is a real person; and it is his great aim that they should do so. God's desire is that men should *remember;* Satan's, that they should *forget.* If men remembered and believed what God has told them about Satan in the Bible, they would be afraid of him, and seek deliverance from him. But they either forget or do not believe it, which is one and the same thing; and in consequence they fancy they are following their own wisdom and their own reason, while they are in reality led captive by a power whose very existence they do not realize.

I do not believe that any man ever yet did anything with no other motive than a simple desire to dishonour God and please Satan. I *say I do not* believe that anybody ever yet did anything with no other motive than one of these. Fancying he is a free agent, man forgets both God and the devil; and does, and leaves undone, as seems wise, or pleasant, or right in his own eyes. Yet for all that—forget it or disbelieve it as he may—man in his natural state (by which I mean man guided and governed by the spirit with which he comes into the world) never does *anything* but dishonour God, and please Satan. He neither knows it, nor sees it, nor feels it, nor believes it: yet it is true—and it has been true of every child of Adam, since Eve was tempted and fell, and man in consequence of her sin was left "*without God in the world.*"

Let us examine this. Who led Eve when she plucked the forbidden fruit? You will at once say, Satan. But did Eve think so, any more than you thought so when you committed your last sin against God? I think not. I do not think that she, any more tha you did, sat down to weigh what God ha said, and what Satan; but that forgettin both, and judging after the seeing of he own eyes and the teaching of her own hear she plucked the fruit, and believed at the tim she was doing a very sensible thing. As Go and the devil have done to you, so had the done to her: God had told her one thing, an the devil another. But I do not believe tha either what God or the devil had told her wer in all her thoughts when she plucked the forbidden fruit. She WAS led by Satan, but sh had no sensible perception of it. The only thing of which she had sensible perception was th evidence of her own senses, and *these* she believed and thought she followed. "*When th woman saw that the tree was good for food, and that it was pleasant to the eyes, and a tree t be desired to make one wise, she took of the frui thereof, and did eat.*" (Gen. iii. 6.) It was not because God said, "*Do not take it,*" *that she took it*, or because the devil said, "*Do take it,*" *that she took it;* but it was BECAUSE SHE SAW THAT IT WAS GOOD. The teacher SELF was the teacher she believed—*but who was the teacher that taught the teacher* SELF?

Reader, it was the teacher who has since then taught all the posterity of Adam to consider that good which God has said is not good—that pleasant which God has said is not pleasant—that to be desired which God has said is not to be desired. It was man's great adversary the devil, who sometimes disguised in sheep's clothing—sometimes transformed into an angel of light,—is going about as a roaring lion, now as then, seeking whom he may devour.

In the moment that she sinned, Eve became Satan's lawful captive. God had said, "In the day thou eatest thereof thou shalt surely die," and the death that God threatened included becoming the property of Satan, and having a portion in the place prepared for the devil and his angels; and in the day she eat, *she did die.* She did not die bodily, but in the day she sinned God left her,—and *to be without God is death*—and in the day that God left her, he who has "*the power of death, that is the devil*" (Heb. ii. 14), took possession of her,—took possession of that spiritually dead heart which was then without God, and which every one of the seed of Adam have inherited from her. I have no doubt that Eve afterwards got a new heart, and was delivered out of the power of Satan; but that was *of grace, through faith*, and not of her own works or deservings. But in consequence of her sin, every child of Adam ever has been, and ever will be born with the heart which Eve had in the moment when she believed Satan,—a heart that is "enmity against God,"—a heart "deceitful above all things, and desperately wicked," —a heart of which Satan was the manufacturer in the day that our first parents sinned, and were left of God.

I must pursue the subject a little further, for there is a soul-destroying heresy abroad, that man is born with a seed of good in his heart. HE IS NOT. God expressly declares, both before and after the flood, that the thoughts of man's heart are evil, only evil, and that continually; and one of the proofs, apart from the decided statements of Scripture, is this,—that you *can* train for a certainty to evil, but you *cannot* train for a certainty to good. Kidnap the child of the most excellent on the earth, and placing it in the haunts of vice, you can train it for a certainty to evil; but let the most excellent on the earth keep his child and educate it, he cannot, as has been proved again and again, train it for a certainty to good. The reason is evident: there is in its heart the seed of evil, but there is not the seed of good; and ground can only be made to produce that of which it has the seed in itself. You might cultivate ground for ever, but unless you put in the seed-corn, it never would produce wheat.

Cain, the first-born of Eve, we are expressly told was "*of that wicked one*," and Abel *by nature* was no better. Abel, Enoch, Abraham, Moses, Peter, James, John, Paul, all by nature the children of Eve, were consequently, as Paul says of himself, all "by nature the children of wrath, even as others" (Eph. ii. 2); and it was only BY FAITH that Abel offered unto God a more excellent sacrifice than Cain—It was only BY FAITH that Enoch pleased God, and was translated.—(Heb. ii. 4, 5, 6.) It was only BY

FAITH—"by faith that is in ME," said the Lord Jesus to Paul, when he was journeying to Damascus,—"in ME, the Son of God, who was manifested that I might destroy the works of the devil" (1 John iii. 8),—that Abraham, or any of that great multitude who were once the children of the wicked one, were ever turned "*from darkness to light*, and from *the power of Satan unto God*." (Acts xxvi. 18.)

Man is not the child of God by nature; he is made the child of God by faith in Christ Jesus (Gal. iii. 27); and all who are not of faith are, as Jesus said to the Jews, of their father the devil. (John viii. 44.) In all those who have not Christ, Satan does his mighty work of madness: so that even while they profess to believe that they are immortal beings,—that there is a God who is to judge them,—a Saviour who can save them,—a Holy Spirit who can sanctify them,—a devil who is destroying them,—a heaven and a hell, in one of which they must live for ever—they get from him a madness that enables them to forget it, and live as if these truths were fables!

"*The Seed is the Word of God,*" says Jesus; "*but when they have heard, Satan cometh immediately and taketh away the Word.*" (Mark iv. 15.) And again: "*The wicked shall be turned into hell, and all the people that forget God.*" Now if for a man to be under the dominion of a power that can take the good Seed of the Word out of his heart,—and when God has Himself declared that he who forgets God shall be turned into hell, can make him forget Him, is not to be in possession of an evil spirit, then man in his natural state is not devil-possessed. But if the contrary is true, MAN IS; and oh, who can describe the power of Satan over that man who, *being in his power, does not believe it—or has power to forget it—or be indifferent about it?*

In conclusion, I would warn man against daring to bring God to the judgment-seat of his own wisdom, for any of the truths declared in this chapter, unless he can prove they are contrary to the doctrines of the Bible; and then the fault is mine. It is the devil that has destroyed man, and not God—and God never made a devil. God made the devil and his angels—*angels;* but they kept not their first estate, and made *themselves* devils. Likewise God made man *in His own likeness, and told him how to keep it*—but man did what he has done ever since,—believed the devil rather than God, and made *himself* a sinner. *God never made a sinner*, neither did He ever make a devil; but sinners, and doubtless devils also, having made *themselves* what they are, would now cast the blame upon God. But the works of God's hands, whether men o: angels, are accountable to God *for what H. made them;* and man has only to remembe: that God made him in *His own Image,* anc then look into his own heart, to convince himself that he cannot be what God made him. Jesus Christ has given us the explanation: "*An enemy hath done this. The tare: are the children of the wicked one, the enemy that sowed them is the devil.*" (Matt. xiii 28, 38, 39.)

But although God never made a devil or a sinner, yet it is a faithful saying, and worthy of all acceptation, that Jesus Christ came into the world to save sinners—and that He casteth out devils with His word. (Matt. viii. 16.) "He is the same yesterday, to-day, and for ever." "His hand is not shortened that it cannot save, neither His ear heavy that it cannot hear." He is as able now to deliver out of the power of Satan as He was when He was on earth; and He is as willing. If you have devils, He will deliver YOU if you will go to Him.

If you refuse to go, do you require anything more to convince you that you have a devil, and are mad?

I re-quote, in concluding this chapter, the words of Solomon, that I quoted at its beginning: "*The heart of the sons of men is full of evil, and madness is in their hearts while they live, and after that they go to the dead.*" This evil—this madness—this eternal death,—is *the birthright* of every child of Adam; and no child of Adam, as such, can ever escape from it. It was too strictly entailed on him by the sin of his mother Eve.

By becoming a child of God, he can escape from it.

A child of Adam can only become a chil of God "*by faith in Christ Jesus.*" (Ga iii. 26.)

"Believe in the Lord Jesus Christ, and thc shalt be saved."

V.

The Recovery.

"And when he came to himself, he said, How many hired servants of my Father's have bread enough and to spare, and I perish with hunger!"

It is a very hopeful evidence that a poor sinner is about to come to himself, when he begins to believe that the servants of God are better off than he is. No man does this by nature. He may say he does. I have heard people again and again say, You Christians are far happier people, and much better off than we are, but they do not really believe it; if they did, they would become Christians. But when a man really in his heart feels what the Prodigal felt when he contrasted his own condition with the condition of his father's servants, he is not far from the kingdom of heaven. Satan never yet taught a man that the people of God were better off than his own people; neither ever yet did the heart of man, in its natural state, find it out or believe it. But when the Spirit of Truth comes—when He Who is stronger than Satan enters into a man—He binds the father of lies, delivers his captive from his delusions, and leads him into the way of all truth. Then the Sun of Righteousness begins to rise in his heart, with healing on His wings; the gross darkness to flee away, and the true Light to shine. Had not a new Spirit entered into the Prodigal, he never would have added to the cry that he was perishing, that the servants of his father had bread enough and to spare.

The thoughts of the Prodigal were now in

a new and a right direction. Formerly they were all on self, now they are all about his father, and the things of his father. Before "*he came to himself*"—whether in prosperity or adversity, whether in search of happiness or relief from misery,—it was to *himself* he looked—to his own notion of things—to his own resources. But now that he had come to himself, his first act was to cease from himself. He knew that he had destroyed himself, but he knew also that he could not help himself,—that there was nothing in, around, or about himself that could save him from perishing. He had brought himself to what he was, but it was no use to keep looking longer at that to which he had brought himself. He was perishing with hunger, and to keep looking at what he had done, or what he was, could not keep him from starvation. At what then was he to look? or what could help him? There was one thing, and but one that he knew of, but to get that seemed impossible. With what bitter agony did he remember it now, for it could save him, and once he had turned his back upon it. What was it? It was THE BREAD that was in his father's house. "*How many hired servants in my father's house have bread enough and to spare, and I perish with hunger.*"

Poor Prodigal! thou hast indeed come to thyself. Thou dost not know it yet; but if thou hadst not, thou wouldst have perished in a vain endeavour to make the very stones bread, before thou wouldst have believed that the bread in thy father's house could save and satisfy thee.

Poor Prodigal! I think I see thee now at the swine-trough, in the moment thou hast come to thyself,—in the moment that it has first burst on thee that thou art perishing, and hast been all thy life deceived, and deceiving thyself. How bitter is thine agony! Who can describe it? Thou art still surrounded by the husks, but thou makest no attempt to feed on them now. Thou hast learned now, not only that they are not food, but poison. Oh, how thou loathest their sight—those husks! Thou once thoughtest them "good things" (better, at all events, than the Bread in thy father's house); but now, were the wealth of the whole world in thy power, how gladly wouldst thou give it, that thou hadst never left the Bread. He who brought thee to thyself, has brought thee to cry from thy heart, "I had rather be a door-keeper in the house of my God, than to dwell in the tents of wickedness."

Poor Prodigal! I believe thou art experiencing the nearest approach to hell that a man can feel on earth. The time passed in passing from darkness to light, from the powe of Satan to God,—the time passed after tho hast been awakened to feel thy need of i before thou realizest thy possession of th Bread that is in thy father's house.

But be of good cheer, poor Prodigal, fo thus saith thy Father—the Lord of Hosts i His name, and thy Redeemer, the Holy On of Israel—"FEAR NOT." It is true thou ar poor, and needy, and hungry, and hast no thing, and art perishing, and hast brought al this, and more than thou knowest, upon thy self; but thy desire is towards thy Fathe and the Bread that is in His house; and thu saith the Lord, "*Blessed are ye that hunge now, for ye shall be filled.*" Thine is th hunger to which this promise is made, an thou art blessed already, and shalt be satisfied

"*How many hired servants of my father's have bread enough and to spare!*"

There is a great truth contained in these first words uttered by the Prodigal after he came to himself.

In a work like this, I do not stop to inquire what, if any, was the difference between the bread the children eat, and the bread the servants eat. I believe, and the Prodigal believed so too, that the bread the servants eat would save him from perishing; and it is quite certain that THE BREAD which I interpret it as representing, is the ONE BREAD of which the whole Christian family partake, and of which if a man eat, he shall never die. Of this Bread every true servant of the Father has enough and "TO SPARE."

Reader, there is a great truth, conveying a great responsibility, contained in these words, "TO SPARE."

Are you a Christian,—one who professes to be of the number of Christ's saved people? If so, call to mind the Christian's song that w quoted so often in the first chapters of thi book: "*Worthy is the Lamb that was slain t receive power, and riches, and wisdom, an strength, and honour, and glory, and blessing.* Remember, too, the conclusion to which w then came,—that he was a Prodigal, and guilt of the Prodigal's sin, who wasted the portio of goods that had fallen to him, and did nc render unto his Father the things that wer his Father's. Now your *Bread to spare* is es sentially your Father's: are you rendering i to Him? If you are of His household yo have it, and it is He that has given it to yo —your *Bread to spare*—for a particular pur pose. He has given it to YOU, *that* YOU *ma give it to the perishing.* YOU have that c which if a man eat he shall live for ever; an I leave you to judge for yourself what h appears in the eyes of his Father who has it, see his brother perishing, and does not offer him it. Do you think the Prodigal at the swine-trough was a more grieving sight to the Holy Spirit of thy Father?

"*Deliver me from blood-guiltiness,*" prayed David; and have not multitudes of Christians need to pray David's prayer? Let us examine ourselves, for I believe the blood of our brother lies on too many of us.

I believe it is in consequence of this sin—because Christians are ashamed of Christ, and do not speak of Him, and tell others about Him, and offer Him to those who they believe to be without Him,—that the world, as a world, continues so much in the power of the wicked one. In one sense Christians are a blessing in the world—a blessing that its people little dream of. They are the salt of the earth, the light of the world; and woe, woe to the world, the day the last Christian is gathered out of it. But for all that, the world has great and just cause of complaint against Christians, because their salt is so often savourless, and the light that is in them so often so very like darkness. They have bread enough, and *to spare;* but instead of scattering it, they keep it wrapped up in a napkin; instead of doing good with it to others, they keep it, as the Israelites did their manna in the wilderness, till it breeds worms, which eat into the vitality of their own souls.

Now the people of the world, simply because they are the people of the world, do not reproach Christians for this, or even seem to see it; though I think that many in their hearts do both; but be that as it may, *God sees it;* and I believe that this very sin against the souls of their perishing brethren, accounts for the half-starved state of the souls of so many Christians. In them is the Scripture fulfilled, " *With what measure ye meet, it shall be measured to you again.*" They do not water, and they are not watered; they do not feed, and they are not fed; they do not scatter, and they are not increased. God is dealing with them in judgment, and leanness is in their souls. And moreover, I think also that were a movement in this direction to begin amongst God's people,—were those who profess to have Christ, to scatter Christ as they have opportunity,—that Christianity itself (what there is of it in the world) would soon be in a more healthy state, and that the "TO SPARE"—the crumbs gathered up from the Master's table, and scattered broadcast beside all waters by His people, would be picked up here and there, very often where least expected, and soon produce a great increase of vital godliness.

Should it be the very smallest of portions no

man can tell what good his "TO SPARE" may do, if given away with his Father's blessing. Oh, ye that name the name of the Lord Jesus Christ, though you have but *a crumb* never be afraid to try and do good with it. Satan keeps many from doing the good they might, and that they have all the will to do, by persuading them they have no power. He keeps them content with looking at, and admiring, and envying others who they see labouring, fully persuaded that it would be useless to attempt any such work themselves. Their own souls they trust are safe, but what could they do for the souls of others?

Now, first, let such remember that they HAVE a "*to spare;*" next, that it is not by might or by power that good is done, but by God's Spirit; and lastly, that "the kingdom of heaven"—that kingdom which they wish to see planted in the hearts of their fellow-creatures, and extended on the earth—is like a grain of mustard seed, which, when it is sown, is the least of all seeds. Let them remember these things, and not be hindered by Satan from sowing this little seed of "the kingdom."

How many have there been, who for years after they became Christians, never seemed to think it possible that they could do anything for Christ—or indeed to know that they were called on to attempt to do it—who afterwards, having by the power of God stirred up the grace that was in them, have done very great things. I will venture to mention one, a dear and intimate friend of my own, now with the Lord Jesus—Hay Macdowall Grant, late proprietor of Arndilly Castle, one of the loveliest places in Scotland, on the banks of the Spey.

I do not think that this little book will fall into the hands of many to whom the name of Hay Macdowall Grant, of Arndilly, is unknown. For the last twenty years his life I knew him well, and for abo twenty years, or certainly for many yea previously, he had been a professing Chri tian. For the first six, however, of our a quaintance, I never saw anything about hi very different from other people. He w quiet and gentlemanly; kind, liberal, and ve courteous; firm about any regulations he ha laid down for the government of his hou and household,—two of which were never allow billiards to be played for money, smoking at any time in any part of h house. At the same time he was indulge to habits he did not altogether approve, r buking them with a shake of the head an a grave smile, and going himself alway early to his room. He was a man in whos presence the most thoughtless would set watch upon his lips, and before whom I neve heard a word spoken that might not have been spoken in a lady's drawing-room. But when I have said this I have said all; for during the six years that I knew him previous to 1855, I never heard him say a word, or saw him do a thing,—or heard from others of his so saying or doing,—that could in any way help the cause of Christ, or lead anybody to suspect he had more religion than his neighbours. Some people I believe will say that the picture I have drawn of him is the picture of what a Christian should be, but I do not think so; on the contrary, I will be bold to state that there is no man who does much more harm to the cause of Christ on earth, than he who has the name of being a Christian, and who neither in his conduct nor conversation, says or does anything that offends those who are not Christians. If this be true Christian life, then is the offence of the cross ceased.

In the end of the year 1854, it pleased God to make me anxious about my own soul; and in a year afterwards, at the end of 1855, I began to speak for Christ. Mr. Grant heard of it, and came to see me; neither as approving nor disapproving, but to see and judge for himself. About the same time a godly brother-in-law, the Rev. Mr. Aitken, arrived from England to visit him, and held many and deeply interesting religious meetings at Arndilly; and shortly afterwards the dumb devil was cast out of Mr. Grant. He whose ears had so long been opened, but whose tongue till then had never been loosened—Mr. Grant, of Arndilly, began to speak for Christ! Two years afterwards, I myself heard him state, at a public meeting in Edinburgh, what had been the visible effects of his speaking for those first two years. He was lecturing on the very subject on which I am now writing,—the necessity of

Christians trying to work for Jesus. "Two years ago," he said, "I think I was a Christian, but I had never attempted to do anything for Christ: I thought it was no use —that I could not—that there was nothing in my power. But two years ago I began to try. In a short time afterwards, a person came to say that what they had heard from me had made them anxious about their soul; and then shortly came another, and then another, and another. I kept their names and addresses, as I have of all who have come to speak to me, up to this day. Last year there came to me between three and four hundred, and this year there have come more than five hundred! Of these nine hundred persons awakened to a sense of anxiety about their souls within the last two years, *I have reason to believe that more than three hundred have been savingly con-*

verted to God, and are now leading Christian lives!"

Dear, dear reader, this is no fabulous story. It is an account of a real work, that I not only heard given by its author with my own ears, but to very much of which I was a witness with my own eyes. In the third year of his work, it was impossible for Mr. Grant to continue to keep a correct list of those who came to speak to him, for they became so numerous that he could no longer receive them singly, but after his services had to speak to them *by rooms full.* Many, many are there in Scotland, and I would mention specially in Aberdeen, who never will forget that *third year*, and who from that time to this, now between eleven and twelve years ago, have been living Christian lives, and blessing God for sending Mr. Grant, with his "*to spare*," amongst them.

I am not writing his biography, but let me take this opportunity of saying that I think it ought to be written. I have merely mentioned Mr. Grant as showing that no man can know what God may enable him to do till he tries, and how that within my own personal knowledge, a Christian who for years either would not or thought he could not do anything for the spiritual good of his fellow-creatures, suddenly arose, went to Christ for help, and did one of the most useful works of his day and generation. Neither will his day and generation end the work that he did. He was not only faithful, but blessed unto the end. In the early spring of this year, 1870, fifteen years after he began to scatter his "*to spare*," living far away from his own comfortable home, in a cottage at Gateshead, where he had gone to supply the place of a dear young Christian brother, while he went abroad for his health, Hay Macdowall Grant preached Christ till he could speak no longer (A FACT!), and then fell asleep in Jesus. But he being dead yet speaketh. The seed that he scattered—his "*to spare*"—is yet bearing fruit that hath seed in itself after its kind, which will bear fruit again and seed again,—that will fruit and seed, fruit and seed, until time shall be no more.

But I have a more encouraging history still to tell to those who are really anxious to do good to their fellow-creatures, and yet feel straightened in their own powers. May it be mixed with faith in you that hear it!

The Lord Jesus Christ was once in a desert place, surrounded by a vast multitude, who had been with Him from morning to near night, and had nothing to eat. There were a few godly men around Him, who seeing their state, became very anxious that the people should get food, lest they should faint on their way home. These men, not having the least idea that THEY in any way could do anything themselves, came to Jesus, and said, "Send the multitude away, that they may go into the villages, and buy themselves victuals. But Jesus said unto them, *They need not depart: give ye them to eat.*"

Consider for a moment, ye who think ye can do little or nothing for Christ, what must have been the surprise of these his true disciples, at hearing these unexpected words. WE give them to eat! We who are here, thirteen of us, in this desert place, and have but five loaves and two fishes, barely enough for our own necessities. Where should WE get bread in the wilderness, that all these may eat? Jesus said, Bring the five loaves and the two fishes to ME, and they brought them: "*And He commanded the multitude to sit down* on the *grass, and took the five loaves, and the two fishes, and looking up to heaven, He blessed, and brake, and gave the loaves to His disciples, and the disciples to the multitude. And they did all eat, and were filled: and they took up of the fragments that remained twelve baskets full. And they that had eaten were about five thousand men, beside women and children."* Matt. xiv. 15—21.

Reader, He is the same Lord still, and the multitude is perishing for want of food still. What He said to His disciples in that day, He says to them in this: "*Give ye them to eat.*" Woe to the man, says Christ, who says he has nothing to give: "*from him shall be taken even that which he seemeth to have.*" (Luke viii. 18.) If you are His true disciples you have bread enough and *to spare;* and as His disciples brought the five loaves and fishes, so bring your crumb to Him to bless it, and then—"give ye them to eat."

VI.

Repentance and Conversion.

"*I will arise and go to my father, and will say unto him, Father, I have sinned against heaven, and before thee, and am no more worthy to be called thy son: make me as one of thy hired servants.*" (Luke xv. 18, 19.)

The Prodigal has indeed come to himself: the enmity has been slain; old things have passed away, and all things have become new. He whose heart had appeared so hopelessly alienated is now occupied with one all-absorbing thought,—how he may be reconciled to his father. "I will arise and go to my father, and say unto him, Father, I have sinned against heaven and before thee, and am no more w thy to be called thy son."

But is reconciliation possible? Had e father been so sinned against, and can ever forgive his Prodigal Son? When had a son's portion, and might have lived a son in his father's house, he preferred gather all together, and go into a far countr there he wasted that portion in riotous livi Then, when all beside was spent, the enmi against his father was not spent, but show itself worse than ever. He was in want, a he had brought it upon himself; but rath than return to his father, who doubtless knew quite well then would have relieved l wants, he preferred to join himself to a citiz of the country in which he was; yea, he to bond-service with that citizen; yea, he we to his swine-trough and fed his swine; ye rather than return to his father and tl wholesome, life-sustaining bread that was in his house, he tried to satisfy his hunger with the husks that the swine were eating. Until he had tried everything and everybody, "*and no man gave unto him*," he never seemed to feel, much less acknowledge the truth, that the lowest servant in his father's house was better off than he was.

But now, brought to the very jaws of destruction, he cries, "I will arise and go to my father," and he did arise and go to his father. The ways of his father are not as our ways, nor his thoughts as our thoughts; and they were reconciled. Of that reconciliation I will speak, God permitting me, presently; but I open this chapter with this brief recapitulation, that I may point out to you, oh, ye young, the misery people bring on themselves, even though in the end they are saved, by wandering away from God; and to you, oh men, young and old, who have wandered from Him, and are still in the far country, that, feel or think about it as you may, you are at *this moment* not one whit better off than was the Prodigal in his extremest need. He was perishing, and so are you; yea, he was better off than you, far better, for *he felt he was perishing, and you do not.* Arise, oh, arise as he did, go to the Father at once, and confess your sin! You are at this moment amongst the perishing, but that is a mercy, compared to what you may be to-morrow: before another day comes you may be no longer amongst the perishing, but *amongst the lost;* amongst those who have rejected God's call *once too often;* amongst those of whom He has sworn in His wrath, that they shall never enter into His rest!

The Prodigal is now a penitent man, showing all the marks of true repentance: and a little further on in the history we learn that he became a converted man; and as I think few portions of Scripture give a better illustration of true repentance and conversion than this part of the history of the Prodigal Son, I will take the opportunity of here saying a few words about both. I do this the more willingly because I believe very great error exists in the minds of many, amounting in multitudes of instances to total ignorance as to what God really means in His Holy Word by REPENTANCE and CONVERSION.

Before I speak about the doctrines themselves, however, let me say a word about their importance.

Surrounded by His disciples, at that time probably the best set of men upon earth, Jesus said, "Except ye repent ye shall all likewise perish;" and again, "Except ye be converted...... ye shall not enter into the kingdom of heaven." (Luke xiii. 3, and Matt. xviii. 3.) Now it necessarily follows that HE who has said, "Except ye repent, ye shall all likewise perish," and "Except ye be converted......ye shall not enter into the kingdom of heaven," IS NOT THE TRUTH if any who die without having repented DO NOT perish, or if any who die without having been converted DO enter into the kingdom of heaven. The destruction therefore of the impenitent and unconverted is as certain as the Word of God is true: HIS TRUTH is pledged for their destruction. Judge then, can anything be more important to a man than to know the real meaning of these doctrines; until he does, how can he examine and ascertain whether he has himself repented and been converted.

Again: a word on the way in which, notwithstanding their importance, these truths have been in all ages and are still received by the great masses of professing Christians. They have known them from their childhood: have known the texts I have quoted above, and that neither the impenitent nor unconverted can be saved; and yet, not only have they neither repented nor been converted, but have remained so utterly indifferent about the matter that they have never as yet seriously set themselves to inquire what repentance and conversion means! If you are one of such Christians, and yet deny the existence of principalities and powers and spiritual wickedness in high places, about which I have already spoken, and against which God tells us we have to wrestle,—*reflect for a moment.* How do you account for the almost total indifference of such multitudes to these things? How do you account for your own? You are not by nature indifferent to your *earthly* interests; how then is it that you to the most important of all your interests your spiritual? Heavenly things are m than earthly, eternal things than tempor and, no matter what you have or who y are, the man who has repented and has be converted is better off than you are. Y know he is: you acknowledge it to yours and wish you were he. Yet, for all th there is a power that you can neither a count for nor control, under whose influen you would rather do anything or nothi than sit down and begin to think seriou about repentance and conversion! Now ho I ask again, do you account for this? Sure you must be possessed by him whose nam is "Legion," if you do not confess that yo and every other such man, has *a devil, a is mad.*

I have known this want of knowledge

to what God really means by repentance and conversion give Satan some most terrible victories. I have known him persuade people who had an imaginary and unscriptural idea of what repentance meant, after by the grace of God they had become anxious about their souls, and made apparently willing to forsake everything for Christ, give it all up again, and go back to the world in despair, because Christ had said, "*Except ye repent ye shall all likewise perish;*" and THEY COULD NOT FIND IN THEIR OWN HEARTS WHAT THEY THOUGHT TRUE REPENTANCE OUGHT TO BE!

Prove every doctrine you hold *not from your heart*, *but from your Bible*, *with prayer to God for the teaching of His Holy Spirit;* and if any man asks you your reasons for your doctrines, be prepared to show them to him in THE BOOK from which you got them. The Bible is the Word of God, "*the faithful* and *true witness*" but out of the heart comes "*false witness;*" and, receive it or not as you may, this truth remains the same,—that the heart of every impenitent and unconverted man is *in the power of the father of lies.* (Matt. xv. 19.)

And now about repentance. Before I try and tell you what it is, let me endeavour to meet that error which I have hinted at above, and which has been such a stumbling-block and cause of despair to so many, and try and tell you what it is not.

It is NOT a certain amount of felt and experienced broken-heartedness caused by the recollection in the penitent of the great wickedness of his past life. The Prodigal confessed his sins, and honestly determined to forsake them; but his first thought was *not* about his sins, but about his father. Many have imagined that there must be emotional and felt sorrow, and that without this there could be no true repentance; and by this error, after having been awakened to a sincere desire to be reconciled to their Father, they have been kept until their convictions have died away, from the only way of reconciliation, because instead of LOOKING AT JESUS they have kept their eyes fixed on what was going on in their own hearts. To get a sinner who is anxious about his soul to do this is the first aim of him of whom I have been speaking so much lately,—Satan. It is not his first aim with the world generally, but it is with an anxious soul. His aim with the world is that they should *forget God;* but when he can no longer succeed in getting a sinner to forget God, his next aim is, that in his thoughts about salvation he should look *at himself and what he feels, and not at God and what He says.* To get a sinner to do either answers

Satan's purpose equally. It is written, "Look unto ME, and be ye saved, all the ends of the earth; for I am God, and there is none else;" and while there is "*life for a look at the Crucified One,*" there is no life for anybody—let *his feelings* be what they may—who seeks to get his hope out of those *feelings*, and refuses to obey the commandment of God,—"*Look unto Me.*"

Christ has expressly told us that the brazen serpent in the wilderness was a type of Himself. The Israelites—bitten by flying, fiery serpents (pictures of ourselves, bitten by sin), —were dying by thousands. "*And the Lord said to Moses, Make thee a fiery serpent, and set it upon a pole, and it shall come to pass that everyone that is bitten, when he looketh upon it shall live.*" (Num. xxi. 8.) Now if a bitten Israelite paid no attention to the bites; thought—as some people do about their sins,—that they were too slight to be worth notice,—that they would cure themselves, or if they did not, would do no harm,—the bites would have been certain to kill him; but so also would they have been certain to kill the man who, alive to all their danger, *kept looking at the bites.* God's promise was, "*when he looketh on the fiery serpent he shall live;*" and it mattered not what kept his eyes off,—if his eyes were kept off the fiery serpent, he died. Just so is it now. The sinner who never thinks anything at all about his being a sinner, but lives and dies in forgetfulness and neglect of God, is sure to perish; but not less sure to perish is the sinner who is kept—even though it be by his religious convictions and anxieties—from believing in Jesus Christ. The mark of faith and obedience in the Israelites was not waiting till they saw certain hopeful appearances in the bite before they looked at the serpent;

the mark of repentance towards God in penitent is not waiting till he finds cert hopeful experiences in his heart before ventures to believe God's Word.

Let no one think, however, I am teachi that emotional and felt sorrow for sin m not accompany true repentance. All I say that it is *in itself* neither true repentance n necessary to it. Nay, more, I am inclined think that although it may, it does not gen rally accompany it. "Surely *after* I w turned," saith Ephraim, "I repented; ar *after* that I was instructed, I smote upon n thigh." (Jer. xxxi. 19.) And I think that th godly sorrow which worketh repentance n to be repented of,—that emotional and fe grief, which after the Lord had looked c him, sent Peter out to weep bitterly,—is n so frequently experienced by the sinner wh in a state of spiritual anxiety, as it is after l has believed in the Lord Jesus Christ, and realized his own forgiveness. I know nothing so calculated to break a man's hard heart, as to see Christ *by faith* at the right hand of God, and to hear Him *by faith* making intercession for him.

Then *what is repentance?* May God the Holy Spirit help me, for the Lord Jesus Christ's great name sake, while I try and tell you; for be it what it may, it is absolutely necessary to salvation.

Μετανοιὰ, the Greek word, and translated in our version "*repentance*," in its plainest and most literal meaning, signifies "*a change of mind*." The text, "Except ye repent, ye shall all likewise perish," would have been better, because more literally translated, had it been rendered, "Except ye change your minds, ye shall all likewise perish." Then what does that mean, you ask again—and again, I pray,

oh God, help me, while I try and answer y
It means that *every man who from his bi
to his grave remains unchanged in the thoug
and opinions that he has by nature about G
shall perish. A change of mind towards G*
was what Paul meant when he preached pu
licly, and from house to house, "*repenta
towards God;*" and it was what Jesus mea
and John the Baptist meant, and all the d
ciples of our Lord meant, whenever th
preached "*repentance.*" "The natural ma
"the fleshly mind," "the carnal mind"—
Scriptural expressions, meaning one and t
same thing,—"*is enmity against God*" (Ro
viii. 7); and repentance is A CHANGE TH.
DESTROYS THAT ENMITY, AND TURNS TI
MIND TOWARDS GOD."

Surely I need not stop to prove that enmi
against God—against the God of the Bib
the God and Father of our Lord and Savic

Jesus Christ, than whom there is no other God—is in the heart of every man by nature. First of all *God says it is*, and therefore it must be—and next man's conduct proves it. No matter how much in every other respect he may differ from his fellows, in this there is never a difference. The first act of every man, and the continued act of every man until he repents, and his mind is changed, is like the Prodigal when he left his father's house, *to go away from God*. No sooner does a child begin to speak, and think, and walk, than with its back to God, and its face set to something that is not God, it begins to wander away down the broad road that leads to destruction. Now man does not by nature follow exactly in the path in which everybody else has walked before him: he has always tried, and is continually still trying every conceivable thing by which he may strike out a new way for himself, and rise above the mass of his fellow-creatures. But there is one way, and it is a new and living way, which no man ever yet tried by nature. No man of his own natural wisdom and reason, ever yet tried to do good to himself, and rise above his fellow-creatures by obedience to the First Commandment: "I AM THE LORD THY GOD; THOU SHALT HAVE NONE OTHER GODS BEFORE ME." There have been instances of men *whose nature was so unnatural*, that by the singularity of their depravity they have brought themselves below the level of the beasts that perish; but there never was an instance of a man *whose nature was so unnatural as to lead him to make God his first object!*

Now repentance—that repentance without which a man must perish, is *a change of mind* that alters all this. A man following the devices and desires of his own heart, hurrying down the broad road that leads to destruction, his mind alienated from God, and his heart covetous and desirous of something that is not God, suddenly begins to think. No matter what makes him think—in the case of the Prodigal, it was that he was perishing—but no matter what the instrument, the man begins to think,—is arrested and stops. Then come the thoughts upon him, What am I doing?—Where am I going?—Whither is the road I am walking in leading me? Every day I am a day older,—a day less of life, a day nearer death; and though this road suits me well enongh just now, I am sinning against God and my own soul, and its end is destruction. I am destroying myself. I will go no further this way. I will turn while there is time, and go to God.

Reader, this is repentance,—it may come with more or less diversity of operation—but it is a true description—*a change of mind, no matter what produces it, that determines a man to forsake sin and his own ways, and turn to God.* When the Prodigal changed his mind about trying any longer to satisfy his hunger with the husks the swine eat, and said, "I will arise and go to my father," his mind was changed—he was a penitent man.

But now comes the question, What is the true evidence of this repentance being genuine? Would it have been for the man suddenly arrested in the broad road, to have sat down and began to cry, because he was not *good enough* to change his mind and turn? I have known many do so, who after very little temptation, were up and off again, and down the broad road as hard as ever. Would it have been for the Prodigal to have contented himself with saying, "I will arise and go to *my father*," and while he moaned and groaned over the destruction he had brought on himself, to have continued sitting with his face to the swine-trough, and his back to his father's house? No: many have got thus far with repentance, who never have been turned to God, or entered into the kingdom of heaven. The only genuine evidence of repentance is CONVERSION.

In the Old Testament the word repentance is seldom used in relation to the sinner. There it is God who is usually spoken of as repenting or changing His mind. The sinner, against whom He has spoken evil, is called upon to *turn*, or be converted, under the promise that if he will turn God will *repent*. The words of God in the Old Testament, "*Turn ye, turn ye, why will ye die!*" are in spirit the same as the words of our Lord in the New: "*Except ye repent, ye shall all likewise perish.*" The man who *turns* will not die, all others will;

the man who *repents* will not perish, all others will. But there can be no turning without repentance, and there can be no repentance without turning. The evidence of REPENTANCE or *change of mind towards God*, is CONVERSION or *turning to God.* And oh, how blessed is that Scripture that maketh the repentance of God CERTAIN to the *turning* sinner: "If that nation against whom I have pronounced *turn* from their evil, I will *repent* of the evil that I thought to do unto them." (Jer. xviii. 8.) As I have said once before in this book, if against a nation, then against an individual.

How fully was the repentance, or change of mind of the Prodigal, evidenced by his conduct! I have said in the beginning of this chapter, that I know no better illustration of repentance and conversion. The Prodigal was sitting perishing—his back to his father's house, and his face to the swine-trough—when the recollection forced itself upon him, "How many hired servants in my father's house have bread enough and to spare!" This recollection produced a change of mind about staying away from his father any longer, and he said, "*I will arise and go to my father.*" This was repentance. In another moment he was a converted, or turned-round man, for we read, "*he arose and came to his father.*" In one instant of time his back was to his father's house, and his face to the swine-trough; in another instant of time his face was to his father's house, and his back to the swine-trough. The repentance of the Prodigal was genuine—it was evidenced by his conduct—*he turned his back where his face was, and his face where his back was*—HE TURNED ROUND.

VII.

The Way Home.

"And he arose, and came to his father." (Luke xv. 20.)

And now the Prodigal has arisen, turned his back upon the swine-trough, and is prepared to go to his father.

But *does he know the way?* Ah, what a question is this! If he does not, neither change of mind about staying away from him, nor genuineness of desire to be reconciled to him, can avail him anything. Unless he knows the WAY, he may wander hither and thither till he perishes. His wanderings will do him no more good than did his seeking to satisfy his hunger with the husks the swine eat. They will never bring him a step nearer his father.

There IS a way back from the far couutry to the Father. Once there was no way; nothing between Him and those who had wandered from Him but *a great wall of separation, with no* DOOR *in it.* While there was no Door, no repentance or change of mind on the part of the wanderer, could be of the slightest use to him. As long as he remained with his back to his Father, it is quite possible that he might know nothing about this wall. I believe there are many unconverted people in the present day who know nothing about it. But it is, and always has been a real wall for all that; and the moment a man changes his mind, and turns round to go to his Father, he finds himself confronted with it. Oh, it is a dreadful wall! No other was ever like it. Its height, its depth, its length, its breath, are beyond measurement. Its top reaches to the heavens. No earthly power could ever get through or over it. Let a man desire, or pray, or turn, or strive as he might, this great wall of separation, if there never had been a Door in it, must always have remained between him and his Father.

But now there is a DOOR in the wall. The wall still remains between the Father and His prodigal sons, as great a barrier as ever; but now there is a DOOR in it, and those who know that DOOR can go through that DOOR, and so get back to their Father.

Of what importance, then, it is that all who have wandered from their Father should know about this DOOR. Oh, ye that know about it, go and tell others! The Prodigal knew about it. We are not *told* he did, but we *know* he did, *because he came to the Father;* for if he had not known about this DOOR, he never could have come to Him. The *very first step* he took after he arose and turned his back on the swine-trough, was through this DOOR; at least, if it was not, all his other steps were labour in vain, and until he did go through the Door, he never got one step nearer his Father. The wall of separation was still between them, and until he went *through the* DOOR, he was as far off the way home as when he was at the swine-trough.

But I believe his very first step *was* through the DOOR. After His son had left Him, the father, at a cost known only to himself, made the DOOR, that all things might be ready if he should ever wish to return; and the same loving Father, the very same against whom he had sinned, so arranged that it was made known to him that there was this DOOR. If He had not, with all his desire, when he came to himself, to go back to his Father, the Pro-

digal would have perished; for though
DOOR would have been there, he
would have found it, and the great
of separation would have remained bet
them.

But he did know about the DOOR. G
and gratitude, and honour, and praise,
thanksgiving, be to the Father who made
DOOR, and revealed it to His Prodigal
"*I will arise*," he said, "*and go to my Fath*
and this change of mind he proved to
genuine, by being no sooner made than
in execution. He arose at once, and tu
his back on the swine-trough. *Immedi*
the wall confronted him; but he had no
then to look at the wall, for in the midst of
wall was an open DOOR, and his eyes
fixed on the open DOOR. His first step
wards his Father's house was off the sw
trough *through that open Door;* and no soo

was he through than the arms of his Father were round his neck!

Reader, the wall is SIN; the DOOR the Lord Jesus Christ. He who gave it to be a Way to Him, is God the Father; and He who showed it to the Prodigal, God the Holy Spirit. Let me say a word about all this, specially to him who wishes to repent, be converted, and reconciled to God.

First of all, about the wall. It is the impenetrable barrier which every man has placed by his own sins, between himself and God: I say every man, because the Word of God says, "*There is no man that sinneth not;*" and again, "*All have sinned and come short.*" And he who has sinned or "*come short,*" has this wall between him and God, and with his own hands has been the builder of it. It is not *the amount of sin.* "In *many things* we offend all," says St. James; but even were it otherwise, and a man could be found wl thought, word, or deed, had only commi *one sin* in his life, *that one sin* would 1 a barrier as impenetrable between him God, as do the sins of the greatest sir in the whole world. To quote St. Ja: again: "Whosoever shall keep the whole l and yet offend in one point, he is guilty all." (James ii. 10.) And he who has o offended in one point, has put a barrier tween himself and God, which no after repe ance or effort of his own can of itself e break down or get over. When God has judge a man in the judgment, the questi will not then be the amount of sin, but "*Gui or not guilty?*" and God, the righteous Jud; cannot pronounce him who has *any sin* up him, *not guilty.*

I beseech you to pray that you may made very clearly to understand about tl doctrine, for the day of judgment IS before you; and it is an error for which you will perish soul and body for ever, if you stand before God on that day with any, *the least sin* on you, and think because it is only *the least sin*, you can escape everlasting destruction. *The least sin* will certainly condemn you. Who then can be saved? Answer: By the deeds of the law, nobody; for by the law is *the knowledge of sin.* You cannot be *saved* by the law, for you have broken it; but looking into it, you see what are its requirements, and *learn* that you have broken it. This broken law—broken by yourself,—is the wall of separation between you and your God.

Again you say, Who then can be saved? By the deeds of the law, nobody; but *by grace*, WHOSOEVER WILL. (Rev. xxii. 17.) You made the wall, but God has made a DOOR through this wall; and Jesus Christ, the DOOR, has put away sin by the sacrifice of Himself. (Heb. ix. 26.) "I am the WAY," says Jesus; "no man cometh unto the Father but by ME." Therefore absolutely the Prodigal could not have gone to the Father, if he had not gone through Jesus Christ. "I am the DOOR," says Jesus: "by ME if any man enter in, he shall be saved." (John xiv. 6; and x. 9.)

How beautifully and clearly, if men had only eyes to see, are these doctrines revealed to us in Scripture. Would that I could point them out to you as clearly. I will try, however, and give you chapter and verse for all I am about to say.

The loving God, knowing that the day was coming in which He must "judge the world *in righteousness*" (Acts xvii. 31), is represented as looking down from heaven to see what was the state of man. Here is the narrative from

His own Word of what He did, and the account of what He saw.

"*The Lord looked down from heaven upon the children of men, to see if there were any that did understand, and seek God. They are all gone aside, they are altogether become filthy: there is none that doeth good, no, not one.*" (Psa. xiv. 2, 3.) This is the testimony given by God Himself, after He had looked down from heaven to see if there were any righteous.

What was to be done? God was not willing that any should perish, but His truth was pledged for the destruction of the wicked; and if they came before Him as they were, no flesh could be saved, for as JUDGE He could not but condemn them. He had said, "The soul that sinneth it shall die," and they had all sinned; there was none righteous —none that did understand and seek after

God—and God is not a man that He should lie—therefore, according to the truth of God, all must perish. But is anything too hard for the wisdom of God, or too self-sacrificing for His love? The first thought of God Himself was, could no way be devised by which He could be a just God and yet a Saviour,—a way by which mercy and truth could meet together,—by which righteousness and peace might embrace each other? "He saw that there was no man, and wondered that there was no intercessor; therefore His arm brought salvation unto him, and His righteousness it sustained him." "God so loved the world, that He gave His only-begotten Son, that whosoever believeth in Him should not perish, but have everlasting life." (Isa. lix. 16; and John iii. 16.)

Now listen. Christ is the Door of which I have been speaking. (John x. 9.) God prepared a Body for Him who in the beginning was with God, and who was God—and in the fulness of the times He sent forth His Son, made of a woman, made under the law, to redeem them who were under the law—and it is a faithful saying, and worthy of all acceptation, that Jesus Christ came into the world to save sinners. (Heb. x. 5; John i. 1; Gal. iv. 4; 1 Tim. i. 15.) He came to live for them and die for them, that by His death and obedience He might work out a perfect righteousness, that might be unto all and upon all them that believe. (Rom. iii. 22.) He came that *He by the grace of God should taste death for every man* (Heb. ii. 9); that whosoever believeth in Him should not perish, but have everlasting life. *For this*, said Christ Himself, *is the will of Him that sent Me, that everyone that seeth the Son, and believeth on Him, may have everlasting life, and I will raise Him up at the last day.* (John vi. 48.)

Now this power to save sinners, the Man Christ Jesus—God manifest in the flesh (1 Tim. iii. 16),—purchased unto Himself thus: First, He magnified God's law on the earth and made it honourable, doing what no other man ever did, keeping both in letter and in Spirit all its commandments. Not one jot or one tittle passed away till all was fulfilled. From His birth to His grave, without ever one moment's failure, He loved the Lord His God with all His heart, and all His soul, and all His mind, and all His strength, and His neighbour as Himself, and this and this only is keeping the commandments of God. This He did however not for Himself, for He had no need, but that sinners who believed on Him and accepted *His obedience as a gift, might* have an obedience imputed to them in which they could stand before God, and be made righteous. (Rom. v. 19.)

But before He could be GOD OUR SAVIOUR, the Man Christ Jesus had more to do than fulfil the law for us, and He did it. "*Himself bore our sins in His own body on the tree.*" (1 Peter ii. 24.) It was not sufficient that man should have a life of sinless obedience to present to God; he had also to get rid of the sins which he had himself committed. Until he did this, the wall of separation still remained, barring, however penitent or anxious he might be, his return to God. But the Man Christ Jesus put away sin too for the sinner. He not only lived for Him a life of sinless obedience, but *He took his sins.* He was *made sin* for him; sin was imputed to Him who knew no sin, and He was treated as our sins deserved, that we might be treated as His obedience deserved.

"He was made sin for us, who knew no sin, that we might be made the righteousness of God in Him." (2 Cor. v. 21.)

Now "Moses describeth the righteousness which is of the law, that the man which doeth these things shall live by them." (Rom. x. 5.) So that the wages of obedience is life, but the wages of sin is death; and as the sinner who believes gets what Christ has earned by His obedience, so Christ got what the sinner has earned by his disobedience. *"The Lord laid on Him the iniquity of us all;"* and the iniquity being laid on Him, He had to receive its wages. The great wall that was between his Father and the Prodigal when he was at the swine-trough, was between His Father and Christ when our sins were upon Him; OUR SINS SEPARATED BETWEEN HIM AND HIS GOD. This is death, dear brother; this is death: to be separated from God.

It is the death the Saviour feared when He prayed in the garden, "If it be possible, let this cup pass from Me."—It is the death the Saviour felt when He cried, "My God, my God, why hast Thou forsaken Me?"—It is the death the Saviour died when He was "without God in the world." The iniquity laid on Him, separated between Him and His God, and wrung from Him the agonizing cry, "My God, my God, why hast Thou forsaken Me."

But the Blood that cleanseth from all sin was flowing at the time, and it had power to prevail. By its power the wall of separation was broken through,—the veil of the temple was rent in twain,—and the way into the holiest made manifest. Through this rent veil—the door He Himself had made—the Man Christ Jesus was the first to enter. "*By His own blood He entered in once into the holy place;*"

and having washed away all the sins that been laid upon Him, "*obtained eternal rea tion for us.*" (Heb. ix. 12.)

"Glory to God in the highest, on earth p good will towards men!" Christ is the V and Christ is the Door; and "by the Bloo Jesus, by a new and living Way, which has consecrated for us, through the vail, is to sáy, His flesh," an entrance has b made through the wall of separation, into very Presence of the Father. (Heb. x. 19,

"*Through the vail, that is to say,* HIS FLES Never again forget the meaning of the wo "THROUGH JESUS CHRIST."

It was the Father who gave the Son, and Son who made the Door. The Son is given, a the Door is made; but by reason of blindn no child of Adam ever yet discovered t Door for himself,—not one of them ever sav unless it was shown to him. Man is born i a kingdom of darkness, and so cannot see the Door. "He walketh in darkness, and knoweth not whither he goeth, because that darkness hath blinded his eyes." (1 John ii. 11.)

But when Jesus ascended up on high, leading captivity—or the great captive-taker, the devil—captive, He received "gifts for men; yea, for the rebellious also, that the Lord God might dwell among them." (Psa. lxviii 18.) Before that, there was no way for God to dwell amongst men. The wall separated the God of love from man, as much as it separated man from Him. But now, as man goes to God through the Door, Jesus Christ,—so God comes to man; and as God the Father gave the Son, and He made the Door, so now for the Son's sake He gives God the Spirit to come through the Door, and take of the things that are Jesus Christ's, and show them to sinners. Without they are shown to him by the

Holy Spirit, no man ever knew or can know them. "*What man knoweth the things of a man save the spirit of man, which is in him?*" asks God; and then adds, "*Even so the things of God knoweth no man but the Spirit of God.*" (1 Cor. ii. 11.) But God will give His Holy Spirit to them that ask Him; and when HE is come, says Jesus, *He will guide you into the way of all truth,* "for *He shall receive of Mine, and show it unto you.*" (John xvi. 14.) It is the fault of every man if he has not the Holy Spirit; for it is written, "Ask, and ye shall have; seek, and ye shall find." And if a man has not the Holy Spirit, it is because he never has asked. He may have gone to Church, and "*said his prayers*" from his childhood, but he has never *prayed;* for there is not a man on earth of whom it has been witnessed in heaven, "*Behold he prayeth,*" whose body is not the temple of the Holy Ghost. (1 Cor. vi. 19.)

Reader, salvation is as free to you as the air you breathe, but there is only ONE WAY of salvation, and that is through the DOOR; and in concluding this chapter, I would just put you in mind of the solemn words of Him who made it: "*Strait is the gate, and narrow is the way, which leadeth unto life, and few there be that find it.*" (Matt. vii. 14.) Now I put you not in mind of this to stumble you, but to warn you. It is broad enough and wide enough to admit you, though you are the greatest sinner that ever lived, if you will go through *naked, and having nothing.* But if you attempt to take with you *anything*—the least bit of sin, or the least bit of your own righteousness—it is altogether impassable. They who go through it must forsake ALL that they have, trusting and looking only to the finished work of the Lord Jesus Christ.

VIII.

The Reception.

"*But when he was yet a great way off, his father saw him, and had compassion, and ran, and fell on his neck, and kissed him. And the son said unto him, Father, I have sinned against heaven, and in thy sight, and am no more worthy to be called thy son. But the father said to his servants, Bring forth the best robe, and put it on him; and put a ring on his hand, and shoes on his feet: and bring hither the fatted calf, and kill it; and let us eat, and be merry: for this my son was dead, and is alive again; he was lost, and is found. And they began to be merry.*" (Luke xv. 20—24.)

How can I write on the words quoted

above? How can I enlarge on them, or hope so to illustrate them as to make them clearer in their teaching, or more soul-comforting in their application? They are Christ's own description of the reception given by the Father to His returning Prodigal. Read it again, oh sinner; and then *feed on it in your heart by faith with thanksgiving.*

"But when he was yet a great way off,"—that is, the moment the Prodigal was on the other side of the wall,—"*his Father saw him.*" It was not that by a great and laborious journey the Prodigal had lessened the distance between himself and his Father, and so by his own toil and trouble brought himself so much nearer home that he came in sight. It was not that he had diminished the distance; but that *the wall of separation* was no longer between them. The moment he was *through the* DOOR his Father saw him.

And what did HE see? or, rather, let us ask first, what, when he looked at himself, did the Prodigal see? Oh, what an object of abhorrence—how he loathed himself when he looked at himself! He had but just risen up, and turned his back upon the far country: he had been driven from it to save himself from perishing: and he had not stopped to wash, or in any way to try and cleanse himself. He was nigh unto death before he determined to go to his Father; and he knew that nothing but the Bread that was in his Father's house could save him; and if before he went he stayed to try and make himself fitter to go, he might never go; before he made himself fit he might perish. So he came off, through the DOOR just as he was; but oh, when he looked at *himself*, his heart sunk within him. No one, he thought, fresh from the horrible pit and the miry clay, was ever in such a mess. And his clothing was as bad as himself,—a bundle of filthy rags, which he gave up even attempting to make cover him; for through them, let him do what he would, the shame of his nakedness was everywhere appearing. Thus the Prodigal saw *himself;* but still he would not, and did not turn back. If he did, *to whom could he go?*

But when the eyes of His Father lighted on him coming through the *Door*, how did he look to Him? In all His wide domains he saw nothing that so pleased Him. Never had He seen, since He was the Father, an object in which His soul more delighted, than when He saw His child, over whom His Holy Spirit had so often grieved—coming, rags and dirt, just as he was,—through the DOOR into His sight. It was His child He saw, and nothing but His child. He thought not of his uncleanness:

He had a Fountain open that would wash all that away. (Zech. xiii. 1.) He thought not of his filthy rags: He had a Robe ready for Him, and "fine linen, clean and white." (Rev. xix. 8.) No matter what he had been, or what he was, He had made all things ready; and out of the abundance of His riches was able and willing to supply all the need of his son. As he passed through the DOOR into His sight, He saw not *what* he was, but only *who* he was: "*But when he was yet a great way off, his Father saw him, and had compassion, and ran, and fell on his neck, and kissed him.*" As soon as he was through the Door the Father saw him—and as soon as the Father saw him He ran. I do not be-believe the Prodigal got one step past the DOOR before the arms of his Father were round his neck; for the lightning's flash, or even thought itself is a sluggard, compared to the speed at which that Father can run to meet a returning Prodigal!

And with the arms of his Father round him, the Prodigal did what he said he would do when he first repented in the far country: he confessed his sin. "*And the son said unto Him, Father, I have sinned against heaven, and in Thy sight, and am no more worthy to be called Thy son.*" But He was not allowed to finish what he doubtless still felt, and had made up his mind to say. I am sure he felt it, but he got no time to utter it; for the Father interrupted, saying to the servants, "*Bring forth the best robe and put it on him; and put a ring on his hand, and shoes on his feet: and bring hither the fatted calf, and kill it; and let us eat, and be merry; for this My son was dead, and is alive again; he was lost, and is found.*"

I cannot attempt to enlarge upon this reception. The faithfulness of the picture rests on the word of Him who is One with the Father, and was recorded that the chief of sinners might know the Heart of God.

Let me, however, try and say a few words by way of application. "*The Father ran.*"—The Father said, "*It is meet we should be merry.*" From what I read in my Bible I feel certain that such is the Heart of the Father towards man, that there is no act of self-forgetfulness into which He will not descend to save, to welcome, and to benefit the returning sinner, if the sinner can only show Him how He can save, welcome, and benefit him WITHOUT SIN. He will not SIN to save the sinner: as saith the Prophet, "*He will not do iniquity*" (Zeph. iii. 5),—but so near and dear to His heart is his salvation, that if he can only show Him how WITHOUT SIN He can save him, He will certainly and cordially save him.

How thoroughly has He proved this to us. "*The Father ran.*"—The Father said, "*It is meet we should be merry*"—and all this to welcome back a poor perishing creature, who had nobody to blame but himself for his misery, and who was returning from the swine-trough. But as I meditated on these expressions, "*The Father ran*," "*The Father said*," and so on, the thought to which I have given utterance above,—"*There is nothing God will not do to save a sinner, except sin for him*,"—came across me. The *running*, and the *making merry*, express more than we would have dared to express if we had not had the parable; but when we turn from parables to facts,—when we read the history of the Lord Jesus Christ, Who *being in the form of God, thought it not robbery to be equal with God*, how that for us men and our salvation He came down from heaven; had a Body prepared Him, that He might be able to suffer what God as a Spirit could not suffer; to be wounded for our transgressions—to be bruised for our iniquities—to be set at nought—mocked—buffeted—scourged—spit upon—to be made sin—made a curse—crucified,—what shall we say about the love of God, which passeth knowledge? He would not SIN to save man—He would not be a Saviour except as a just God; but anything except sin,—any abnegation of self,—the whole history of God, as recorded in the Bible, proves to us that He was willing to do and suffer, that He might bring man back *to what He made Him and to what he ought to be.* He would not SIN for him. For *a single bow* the devil offered Him the whole world: that world on which His heart was set, and to save which He lived and died. "*All this will I give Thee,*" said the tempter, "*if Thou wilt fall down and worship me.*" A bow would have done it, and it must have been a GREAT temptation. The agony and bloody sweat, the cross and passion, the death and burial, the patient waiting ever since upon God until He gives Him the heathen for His inheritance, and the uttermost parts of the earth for His possession, would all have been saved Him for *a single bow.* But it was written, "*Thou shalt worship the Lord thy God, and Him only shalt thou serve;*" and to have redeemed men out of the hands of Satan by *a bow,* would have been to have redeemed them by SIN. Had they never been saved till that bow was made, they never would have been saved at all. He will run to meet the returning sinner; He, in conjunction with the whole hosts of heaven, will rejoice and make merry to receive him amongst them; He will do anything and everything, as recorded in the revelation of God and history of Jesus

Christ, to save him; but—*He will not sin* for him.

Reader, think of this. Think of His love, and think of His truth. He would die to save you, but He will not sin to save you. Oh, may His love melt you; but if it does not, then think of His truth. The fear of the Lord is the beginning of wisdom, and if you are still amongst the fools that perish, may it be made so to you. If you die impenitent, unconverted, and without having gone through Jesus Christ, the Door, to God, can He save you unless He sins? He once said to the Jews, If I say thus and thus, "I shall be a liar." (John viii. 55.) Would He not be "a liar," if in such a case He saved you? Some may say that God might do for them many pleasant things, and save them from many trials without sin, but they greatly err. If they are God's children all things are working *together* for their good, and they are in the best position in which He can place them. It would be sin in a father to spare his children sorrow or to give them pleasure to their hurt. If God's children would only remember this, how it would take the sting out of trial.

And now, in conclusion, let me say a few words to some of the different classes who may perhaps be amongst my readers. And first to you whose faces are still toward the far country. To you, thus saith the Lord: "Turn ye, turn ye: why will ye die?" Unless you turn, you *must* die, for the truth of God is against you, and is pledged for your destruction. But see Zech. i. 3: "Thus saith the Lord of hosts; Turn ye unto Me, saith the Lord of hosts, and I will turn unto you, saith the Lord of hosts." This is as true as, "Except ye repent, ye shall all likewise perish;"

and if you will only turn to Him, not only the Truth but the WILL OF GOD will be on your side, for He is NOT WILLING that any should perish. Judgment is His "strange act," and He doth not willingly afflict the children of men (Is. xxviii. 21, and Lam. iii. 33); and if you will only turn, it is not too late for you yet to escape the judgments and afflictions that are most certainly coming on the impenitent and unconverted.

What the Lord Jesus Christ once said to Jerusalem, God now says to every unconverted man who calls himself a Christian: "How often would I have gathered you, as a hen gathereth her chickens under her wings, and ye would not." (Matt. xxiii. 37.) At any moment of your past life, He would have saved you, if you would have been saved; and now is another moment of offered salvation. Be wise and neglect it not. You yourself think that the day must come when you will have to forsake all that stands between you and Christ; for surely you have neither deliberately made up your mind to sell yourself to Satan for what sin and the world can give you, nor to be damned, if the Bible is true. You do intend at some time or other to turn, and you think that time will come; only your heart says, *Not to-day*. But why should it not be to-day? God says, "NOW is the accepted time, NOW is the day of salvation;" and while it is quite certain that if you NOW turn to God through Jesus Christ, God will turn to you and save you; it is also quite certain that if you attend to the wishes of your heart, and Felix-like put it off to a more convenient season, that you never may, and very likely never will turn at all, and consequently never will be saved. If people are to meet they must agree upon the time of meeting as well as upon the place: and God has fixed both the one and the other for His meeting with the sinner. The place is the Cross of Jesus Christ: the time IS NOW. And the Holy Ghost saith, "To-day if you will hear His voice, harden not your heart." If you will attend to what the Holy Ghost saith, and NOW—to-day, while it is called to-day—change your mind, as the Prodigal changed his at the swine-trough, and arise and go to your Father, the Father will receive you as He received the prodigal. "Though your sins be as scarlet, they shall be white as snow; though they be red like crimson, they shall be as wool." (Isa. i. 18.) The Father Himself says of all who so come to Him, "Their sins and their iniquities will I remember no more." (Heb. viii. 12.) But if you put it off, you do so at your peril: and if you do put it off, you may remember this day, and this moment, and this book in hell. It may be your last call, and God may swear in His wrath that you shall never enter into His rest.

But besides the selfish motive of your own salvation, there is another consideration I would urge on you. Think first how good the Father has been to you: how, in spite of all your past, He has borne with you, and is still bearing with you; is even still willing, yea even beseeching you to be reconciled. (2 Cor. v. 26.) Then think, if you will turn now—to-day, at once—of the joy it will give THE FATHER. HE, and all His, from the least to the greatest in the kingdom of heaven will rejoice over you. There is joy in heaven over one sinner that repenteth; and more than that, unless you stop its course of unbelief, that joy shall communicate itself from heaven to you. "Faith is the *substance* of things hoped for, the evidence of things not seen" (Heb. xi. 1), and only arise and go to God through Jesus Christ, and believe your reception to be what He has Himself told you it will be, if you so come to Him, and *by faith* you shall feel as did the Prodigal, the arms of your Father around your neck, and hear His voice welcoming and rejoicing over you. Do you think the loving, rejoicing spirit of the father did not communicate itself to his son. Believing his acceptance from his word and deed, and knowing that his arms were around him, do you think it did not make him very happy?

And why should not you, if you are one who have never yet arisen and gone to the Father, feel this very night when you lie down in your bed what the Prodigal did on the night of his reconciliation? What is to hinder you? Is there anything in the Bible? You know *there* is not. If you will now turn from sin and go to the Father, there is nothing between you and the reception of the Prodigal but the teaching of your own heart, which is enmity against God, and contradicts the Bible. If, going to God, you were to lie down to-night with that in your heart which was in the Prodigal's, your own heart would surely tell you you were presumptuous, self-deceived, and God-dishonouring; but if you held on by the Word of God, and made your heart a liar, you would be the subject of a Christian experience—a grace of God—than which few bring greater glory to Him, or would be more likely hereafter to make you a useful Christian. It would not be presumption,—it would be "*joy and peace in believing*."

And now a word to you who say you have turned your back upon the far country, have arisen and gone to your Father. Are you holy? Are you stirring after it,—perfecting holiness in the fear of the Lord? They to whom much has been forgiven, love much, and love shows itself in service: "Not every one," says the Lord Jesus, "who saith unto Me, Lord, Lord, shall enter into the kingdom of heaven; but he that doeth the will of my Father which is in heaven." Now the will of His Father is our sanctification (1 Thes. iv. 3), and to strive after sanctification is an uphill, self-denying work; but it is a work entailed on every Christian soldier, and a work that entails conflict. The Prodigal at the swine-trough was a slave; the Prodigal restored to his Father's family was a soldier, enlisted to fight manfully against the world, the flesh, and the devil. The same is the case with you; and if you are with steadfast purpose of heart trying to cleave unto the Lord, nobody knows better than you do, that not only externally in the world but internally in your own heart, there is that which terribly tries your holiness. Now are you resisting, in the strength of the Lord, these enemies of your Father and your own soul? You know: I do not; but if you are not, what Scriptural warrant have you for thinking yourself a Christian? You are not to despair, or even be cast down in the conflict because you find yourself a sinner,—but you are to be cast down, and stand in very great doubt of yourself indeed, if you do not find yourself fighting against sin. You will never be good in this world, therefore do not think you are not a Christian because you do not find yourself what you wish to be; but you are *to strive to be good* in this world, because *God has told you to strive;* therefore do not think you are a Christian if you are not striving. "By their fruits ye shall know them," says the Lord Jesus; and "Faith without works is dead." Without the work internal especially, by which we produce instead of th works of the flesh the fruits of the Spirit faith is certainly dead, and in the work external, let us be careful to be forward as we have opportunity; remembering "*Give ye them to eat*," and that "pure religion and undefiled before God and the Father is this, To visit the fatherless and widows in their affliction, and to keep himself unspotted from the world." (James i. 27.) All those recorded in the twenty-fifth of Matthew as lost, were lost not for what they did, but for what they did not do.

But you say you have arisen and gone to your Father, and cannot deny to yourself that you have some evidence of hatred to sin, and strivings after holiness. Jesus is precious to you, and you would not give up your hope in Him, such as it is, for the whole world. But you are not happy. You have nothing of that joy you see others have, and know you ought to have. Then why not? If you really have arisen and gone through Jesus Christ to the Father, and if what I have said above is true of you,—I see no reason to doubt it,—you have *already* received the reception of the Prodigal son. That you say you have not felt it makes no difference: your feelings cannot alter the truth of God. YOU HAVE RECEIVED IT. His arms have been around your neck; nay more, are around you still; so firmly, so securely around you, that none shall ever be able to pluck you out of them. The best robe has been put upon you; the ring, the shoes, and *He in whose presence the angels stand*, has rejoiced over you. But although all this has really and actually taken place, and you are as safe in the Everlasting Arms as ever was the Prodigal, you have never rejoiced over yourself, or realized the fact of your own forgiveness and acceptance.

Now why is this? St. Paul says, "Rejoice in the Lord alway, and again I say rejoice;" and why are you not obeying the command to "Rejoice in the Lord"? Who gave you the Spirit that has led you to go to the Lord? Who gave you the Spirit that makes you fight against and hate sin, though you do not overcome it as you wish to do? Who gave you the Spirit of prayer? Did you not go this very morning to God, and ask Him for Jesus Christ's sake to forgive you your sins, and give you His Holy Spirit? You say, Yes: then why are you not rejoicing in the full belief of your pardon? What answer does God tell you He will make to the prayers of poor sinners who go to Him through Jesus Christ? Does He say He will forgive them, or does He say He will not? You answer, He says He will; and yet add in the same breath, you dare not say He has forgiven you.

What is God, if a man dies without repentance, and does not perish? You say, A liar: what is God, if a man goes to Him through Jesus Christ, and He does not save him? You know that He must be the same: and yet you prefer the teaching of your own heart, and to make God a liar, rather than to believe like a child, and rejoice in His great salvation.

Ah, dear brother, all this is great sin, most dishonouring to God, and hurtful to your own usefulness as a Christian: it is *unbelief*. The remnants of your old nature in enmity against the doctrines of free grace. God's salvation is *of grace;* and if you have ever really been to Him through Jesus Christ, He gave it you the moment you went to Him. You yourself say and know that salvation is only *of graec;* but you will not take it as only *of grace.* You do not rejoice in it, because you can find nothing in which to rejoice, *except grace.* You have been going to God for weeks, or months, or years perhaps; and during the whole of that time, instead of taking what you find in the Bible, you have been looking *into your heart* to find something in which to rejoice. If you could find there what you think you ought to find, whether it be faith, or love, or good works, or what not, you would rejoice; but would that be *rejoicing in Christ?* Would it not rather be rejoicing in one of the most soul-destroying of all sins—"*confidence in the flesh,*" *self-righteousness?* "Aha, I am warm, I have felt the fire," would at once be your cry; and the already too-little-believed in Jesus would be dethroned altogether, and the idol of self-righteousness set up in His place. "We are the circumcision," says Paul, "who worship God in the Spirit, rejoice in Christ Jesus, and have no confidence in the flesh." (Phil. iii. 3.) And it would be better for you to remain a doubting, desponding, little-faith Christian all your life, than to get an increase of what you might think faith, and hope, and joy out of anything you found in yourself.

But though that be true, why should you remain a doubting, desponding, little-faith Christian? You have arisen like the Prodigal, and through Jesus Christ, the Door, gone to your Father, and said, "Father, I have sinned." If so, you have received the Prodigal's reception: for God changeth not. Jesus Christ is the same yesterday, to-day, and for ever: He casteth out none; and the same Lord over all is rich unto all that call upon Him. What would you think of the Prodigal, if in the end of his history, you had read that he sat at supper before his father with a countenance, or even a heart full of despondency? What would you think if, in reply to "Son, what aileth thee: thou art not happy?" the son had answered, "Oh, father if I was sure thou hadst forgiven me I should be so happy; but I am not happy, because I am not sure thou hast forgiven me." Can you conceive anything that would have more checked the joy and rejoicing in the father's heart? It would not have quenched his love: he would not have sent his son back to the far country; but as long as that feeling lasted the father and the son could have had very little happiness together.

This is exactly what you are doing, ye doubting, desponding Christians, who having gone to God through Jesus Christ, refuse to hear His voice saying unto you, "*Be of good cheer, thy sins be forgiven thee.*" (Matt. ix. 2.)

Three questions, and I have done. Are the doctrines contained in this little book calculated to make men happy?

Are the doctrines contained in this little book calculated to make men holy?

Can you disprove them from the Bible?

May God the Spirit, for the Lord Jesus Christ's sake, bless His own Truth, and let nothing that I have said contrary to it do any harm.

Brethren, pray for us.

"The Lord bless thee, and keep thee. The Lord make His face shine upon thee, and be gracious unto thee. The Lord lift up His countenance upon thee, and give thee peace." AMEN.

LONDON:
WILLIAM HUNT AND COMPANY,
HOLLES STREET, CAVENDISH SQUARE.

CPSIA information can be obtained
at www.ICGtesting.com
Printed in the USA
LVHW040737020323
740708LV00002B/216

9 783382 112578